CROSSING WITH THE CAPTAIN

Ten years ago, Libby Grant and Drew Muldoon dated for six months. Despite a string of disasters, they became engaged — then Libby broke up by letter while Drew was at sea. Now on a leisure cruise around Spain and Italy, she discovers to her horror that Drew is the captain of the ship. Can they work through their past problems and rekindle the spark and hope of their old relationship? Or will the mysterious thefts and hacking incidents on board the ship throw a serious spanner in the works?

Books by Judy Jarvie
in the Linford Romance Library:

PITCHED INTO LOVE
SECRET BILLIONAIRE
KILTS AND HIDDEN CRUSHES
OFF LIMITS LOVER

JUDY JARVIE

CROSSING WITH THE CAPTAIN

Complete and Unabridged

LINFORD
Leicester

First published in Great Britain in 2017

First Linford Edition
published 2018

A catalogue record for this book is available
from the British Library.

ISBN 978–1–4448–3615–8

Published by
F. A. Thorpe (Publishing)
Anstey, Leicestershire

Set by Words & Graphics Ltd.
Anstey, Leicestershire
Printed and bound in Great Britain by
T. J. International Ltd., Padstow, Cornwall

This book is printed on acid-free paper

1

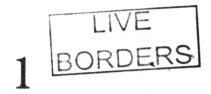

Mediterranean Perfection Cruise, Day Two — Today's To Dos

1. Eat sensibly at lunch. (Recompense for last night's caramel cheesecake at dinner. High-calorie but worth it.)
2. Email Chrissie, watch a movie then visit the piano bar.
3. Save final book chapters to read tonight at the back of the boat under the stars. (This time take a blanket.)
4. Avoid Captain Muldoon. Low profile, keep vigilant. If spotted, vacate area immediately.

Libby Grant smiled as a knock sounded on her cabin door. She replaced the cap on her pen, pushed her to-do list into her bag and rose to answer.

'Come on, Libby! We're on a tight deadline for lunch. If we don't move fast there'll be a line at the salad bar.' Edna Randall's distinctive voice grew louder as the door opened to reveal her diminutive form clad in an aquamarine trouser suit.

Libby teased, 'Edna, we're on a vacation. Not a conveyor belt.'

'It still always pays to get in first,' Edna countered.

Libby laughed lightly. 'I meant we can relax. All the restaurants are all-inclusive service, and there's enough for everyone. Rest assured, it'll be fine.'

Edna stared hard, undeterred. 'Walt's gone to bag a table. We want the best sea vista view too.'

Despite the fact that Libby had a soft spot for her new cruise cabin neighbour acquaintances, Edna and Walt Randall, she figured this seventy-year-old lady must have 'do it my way' as her life motto. Fortunately her kind, attentive husband Walt smoothed the feathers Edna ruffled. And meanwhile, he

2

entertained Libby with his New York smart-talk charm.

Since meeting the pair, she'd realised her resolve to have a quiet, peaceful vacation-of-a-lifetime might not work out that way. But Edna and Walt were being caring over controlling by keeping her company. Libby grabbed her purse and key card with a smile.

'Okay, the view. I get it now. So much ocean, so little time. I'd planned to take a walk after lunch. Fancy a quick promenade later?' Libby encouraged.

But Edna stared at her as if she'd announced she was suggesting she might leave forever in a helicopter for a life of luxury with a wealthy oil sheikh. 'Lunch is only the start of what we've planned — the itinerary is arranged and we have VIP passes for the afternoon, so you need to hurry. There's no time for walking.'

'What have you lined up, Edna?' Libby dared to think. So far she'd already committed herself to daily boules, beginners' tai chi, and a culinary crash course in canapé preparation for the busy hostess. All of which had been instigated by Edna.

'We'll have lunch and then a tour.' Edna clasped her hands in joy. 'Walt won't hear of you dropping out, so we'd better speed up.'

A buzzing noise grew louder nearby as Walt Randall's electric wheelchair appeared in the doorway. His smile melted the frost that had shrivelled Libby's heart with his wife's insistence. Edna pounced on her husband. 'Why aren't you keeping us that table, Walt?'

He smiled back. 'Taken care of, thanks to my favourite waiter friend. I always tip well; pays dividends when you need favours.' Walt waggled his eyebrows and grinned. 'Hey Libby, you'll join us on the tour, won't you? It'll be an amazing afternoon.' Walt Randall's easy, breezy American charm contrasted sharply with his wife's bossy domineering. 'A tour, then high tea. I hear the meringues are outstanding! Wouldn't wanna miss those.'

His tone reminded her of Bing Crosby in *High Society*, and she'd no idea why that popped into her head. Other than the fact that her beloved Aunt Joss had dearly loved Bing's smooth tones. It caused an ache in her heart remembering the loss of her beloved relative, which she was still processing.

'Okay, Walt. I'll do it just for you. Though you'll owe me one.'

'Atta girl, kid!'

Libby ventured, 'In future these itineraries need to get my approval in advance. If either of you dares to enlist me for belly-dancing lessons, it'll be curtains for our friendship.'

Had her godmother been on this trip with her, as they'd planned, she'd be forcing Libby to push her boundaries too. She'd be encouraging her to sample meringues and ignoring the calories.

'Let's get movin'; Pedro won't keep that table forever.' Walt stared hard at her. His checked jacket and matching pants were at odds with his newly acquired Crystal Queen Cruises baseball hat. He blinked glacier-blue eyes, and Libby blinked back. Walt grinned. 'Big ship like this offers plenty of opportunity to chart new courses. Imagine the fun you'll have before we're through.'

Walt had a point. But she also guessed being bossed around was exactly what she'd moved on from. David had done too much of that. By the end he'd run her diary and her likes and dislikes to the point that she'd lost herself along the way. She was only recently free and emerging from old habits since she no longer had David as her controlling force. But now her godmother couldn't steer her right either.

Libby sucked in a breath as she locked her cabin and they headed down the corridor. 'Please don't say it's touring the engine room. Or ask me to prove myself on that climbing wall on the main deck. So what's it to be? A tour of the wine cellar? The spa?' Libby tucked her mobile phone in her bag.

'Better,' Walt stated.

Edna interrupted, 'Captain Muldoon will give us the full VIP tour. A captain's helm tour with high-class tea in his office. I'm wearing my stretch pants especially and hoping for a captain selfie. The girls at my aqua Pilates class will go wild over him. He's divine.'

Libby's inner glow faded on fast freeze at the words, and her chest seized as oxygen left her lungs. She stopped in her tracks. 'Captain Muldoon?' she checked.

'Yes. Of course dear. Who else?'

'He'll lead the tour in person then?'

'He is our esteemed captain.' Edna tutted.

Libby felt her brain spin at this revelation. 'I can't go with you. It's not doable.'

Edna balked and stared. 'Nonsense. Of course you can. We already booked you in.'

Libby heard the tremor in her voice. 'You don't understand. Captain Muldoon and I . . . have shared history.' Libby's fingers flew to her lips. Her brain felt like it had stalled and needed a jump start. 'We aren't strangers. Ten years ago we dated.'

If she'd known prior to booking her cruise that Drew would be their captain, she'd have cancelled, no question. Their six-month relationship had nosedived thanks to awful jinxed dates and a messy break-up. 'I can't face him,' Libby insisted.

'Of course you must,' Edna challenged, seizing Libby's hands in her firm grasp. 'You shall face this fear. He's only a man — what can be so bad? You're a big London corporate lawyer — surely you aren't backing down?'

'Work's easy, Drew is different,' she whispered. She heard her own voice tremble and went on to explain. 'I was barely nineteen, and I jumped ship on our relationship. Seeing him again would be excruciating. For us both.'

Edna clucked with her tongue. 'All the more reason to shed the guilt. Fate has brought you this opportunity, and you should go — apologise, move on. It's kismet.'

'I'm still not doing it,' Libby faltered.

'We'll help you. Why, Walt and I would never have stood a chance if I'd been a shrinking violet about misunderstandings.'

Libby tried again to communicate her reticence. 'Edna, neither of us would rush to revisit the past.'

'Make peace,' Edna stated baldly. 'Destiny calls you to do this.'

Walt looked between them, his eyebrows knitting at their exchange. He shrugged. 'Let's get moving. Do you ladies want a sea view or not? I'm outta here.'

If she'd realised she'd have to come face to face with Drew, she would definitely have made alternative plans. On a ship with over two thousand passengers and staff aboard, Libby had worked out the chances were high of keeping a low profile. But now she had to face the ex-fiancé she'd broken up with by letter and left while he'd been at sea.

'He ruined my favourite outfit, making me wait in the rain. It was silk.'

'Petty mistake,' Edna dismissed.

'Smashed my mother's antique tea service. Then lost my cat on purpose,' Libby whispered, even as Edna walked her along the corridor towards the elevator. 'Sookie was gone for a month and it made her scared to go out.'

Edna waved a hand. 'There must have been a logical explanation.'

Libby closed her eyes as the memories replayed in her mind. 'I wrecked his car by accident; he thought it was revenge.' In truth she'd almost killed his mother, but that was another story involving half-defrosted food. It made her toes curl to recall the list of horrors. In summary, Drew Muldoon would not be over the moon to say hi.

Edna scowled as the elevator pinged open, then pulled Libby inside and waited for Walt to join them. 'He won't remember. Prove you're the better woman here.' She pressed the button and the doors closed. 'Show him what he lost.'

Libby preferred to opt for a lifeboat.

Walt, who'd been listening and watching the whole time, looked at her levelly and simply said, 'Way I see it, any guy who lost you lost out. Won't hurt this one to notice what a sweet dish you are, will it? He might be the boss, but he can still be shown a thing or two.'

Her heart warmed. Something about Walt made her want to hug him and keep him as a friend forever, despite the age gap. But Libby still wasn't convinced by the positive spin. Mostly because at heart she'd regretted her rash ending with Drew ever since. He hadn't deserved it.

Libby breathed deep. 'I hope he doesn't push me overboard.'

'As if we'd let him,' said Edna. 'You're being melodramatic.'

'He tries anything, I'll stop him with my karate,' Walt countered. 'I still have the belts and the moves.'

But walking out of the elevator towards the restaurant, Libby hoped hard Captain Drew Muldoon would feel more amenable about a surprise reunion than she did. Somehow she doubted it.

* * *

Libby decided this must be how the Christians felt nearing the pacing lions. Every step closer made her more nervous, but she straightened her spine and forced herself on; she was an experienced lawyer, she knew daily challenge. So where was her trademark unflappable professionalism now?

But then she had no power suits today. Libby's casual white linen trousers and pale blue cotton blouse attire weren't exactly 'dressed to impress'. She pushed on, ignoring the dissenting voices in her head.

'Good afternoon,' said a female officer with a smile as they passed. She headed in the opposite direction from their pilgrimage to the helm.

Libby gulped, then went for another last-ditch escape plan. 'I may go back and fetch my jacket.'

'You'll do nothing of the sort,' said Edna, and she clutched Libby's arm tight. 'We can't delay further.'

At the elevator she and the Randalls looked for their escort's arrival. A young man in white uniform waited nearby and smiled in greeting; an escort was required to take them to the level where only ship's personnel were permitted.

'Mr and Mrs Randall? May I take you to the bridge?' He led them to ascend to the action deck. Once there, and graciously putting up with Edna's chatter the whole time, he led on and through a door marked 'PRIVATE. Ship Officers.'

Now only the steps to the bridge stood between Libby and her fate. If her best friend Chrissie had been here, she would have pushed her in there with a stern warning of, 'Bluff your way big time.'

Libby sucked in air seeing the rear view of two tall officers against a breath-taking view. There was deep wide sea everywhere through expansive surround windows that showcased ocean from an impressive height, framed by a dazzling sky.

'Wow,' Libby whispered, utterly taken aback by the beauty before her.

Even viewed from behind at a distance, these men in white also had great rear views. But she couldn't discern which of them Drew was yet.

'I need to go!' Libby turned away before any of the officers on the bridge could see her. 'Please apologise. Not feeling good. Must be seasick.'

'But that's nonsense. The modern boats all have stabilisers,' Edna asserted, making Libby realise the woman was too well-read for her own good. Edna shook her head to get her back on course, but Libby wouldn't comply.

She grabbed the escorting officer's arm. 'May I go, please? I need to use the restroom. Can you escort me back?'

'Certainly.' Though he looked a little startled at her urgent request. Libby's heart drummed fast at her impromptu antics, but nothing was going to make her endure this tour.

Ignoring Edna's quizzing questions and Walt's shouts of 'Hey Libby, we'll wait for ya, honey,' she walked fast back through the private door towards the corridor.

'Miss? Are you quite well?' the escort asked.

'I'm fine. Just a little dizzy.'

In the nick of time, a ladies' brass plaque appeared. She moved to make a dash there, but before she could reach it, another door nearby opened swiftly with a click. Within seconds a tall male figure stood stock-still before her, watching her intently. And he was one she'd never mistake.

'Hello, Drew,' she whispered.

'Hi, Libby.' Captain Drew Muldoon's gaze met hers with open shock. He rallied and donned the signature handsome smile of a man she'd find hard to ever forget. 'I can't believe it; Libby Grant.'

'Captain Muldoon. Same to you.'

His blue eyes sparkled like the ocean waves he mastered. His white uniform dazzled even without the gold stripes or the dark-as-night hair. He was dressed for a movie, his uniform displaying broad shoulders that were as impressive as his clean-shaven good looks. Plus his profile put the smoulder in a decade older.

'Of all the ships in all the world,' he said softly.

'My first cruise, and what do you know,' she whispered. Now that the escape plan was blown, all she could do was bluff. 'Nice ship, Drew. Great to see you again.' Libby felt her face flame.

'I trust you're okay?' he asked. The genuine concern on his face made her feel even worse than she did already.

'I'm fine.'

'Enjoying the trip?'

'Yes, so far. And all the sights are yet to be seen. The ship's magnificent.'

'Thanks. It's not really mine; it's only on loan.' He smiled to indicate he was joking.

The escort's voice intruded on their exchanges. 'This passenger complained of feeling nauseous, Captain.' Libby figured maybe he was worried she might have a relapse.

'I can summon our medic from the sick bay,' Drew said, looking quickly concerned.

'Not necessary. A splash of water and I'll be fine, thanks.'

'For a minute I thought you were lost, or trying to escape,' Drew remarked, and the statement shrivelled her pride. He was no fool and probably had her all worked out.

'She's looking for the restroom before the tour starts,' said her escort.

Drew's gaze seared her soul with its

intensity. 'Then I won't detain you. But I hope to welcome you back to the bridge in due course. I'll delay the tour until you're ready. Please don't rush.' And then Drew turned as if to go but lingered for a second longer. 'How are you, Libby?' He watched her intently. 'Still the top lawyer with all the answers?'

Right now she felt like all her thoughts were in a tangle and her conversation skills had flopped. She smiled through it. 'I try. Still mad about rugby and addicted to late-night chess?'

A slice of a smile lit his face. 'My favourite pizza toppings are still the same too; hard to change good taste. You still like veggie special extra mushrooms?'

'Is there any other kind?'

His smile drifted, and it was as if his captain's guise returned in full force. They both turned to see the escort watching them as if uncertain what to do. So Drew seized control. 'We'll catch up another time. See you later, Libby.'

Drew Muldoon pivoted on polished shoes and left her. But Libby couldn't resist watching as he disappeared from view and the escort coughed lightly beside her.

Libby ducked inside the lavatory and shoved her back against the door. She'd got their awkward meeting over with — so why was she still squirming and feeling like wild buffalo were stamping in her ribcage?

She splashed water on her temples with shaking fingers. She'd cruised into a bay of past regrets, then got marooned. And Libby knew the only person responsible was herself.

2

Drew Muldoon excused himself from the passenger in mauve chiffon with the towering jewelled hair. Her rundown on every staff member who'd excelled to make this cruise her most sublime experience yet had been substantial. But Mrs Winterhouse was a loyal customer who deserved attention. Customer care was vital, and contact with the captain was part of the vacation dream. A happy ship meant happy customers meant repeat bookings.

'So gratified to hear that, Mrs. Winterhouse.'

'You really run a very tight ship, Captain.'

'I'm lucky to have a wonderful crew.' Right now he itched to scram. But polite and patient were all part of the job. 'Your loyalty and continued support are much appreciated,' he concluded.

Yet all he could think about was Libby. Here. On board his ship. On vacation yet evading him.

Being on the bridge of *Oceana Onyx*, with open sea and destination on the horizon, a docking in the offing, were his favoured pursuits. Yet when he issued an invitation to dine at the captain's table and the guest declined, pleading that she was unwell, he wasn't used to the slight.

Why would Libby hide? She'd evaded him on the tour. Why did she clam up every time he tried to lure her into conversation? Was she sick? She'd looked fine earlier.

Drew answered his phone on the first ring. 'Muldoon.'

'Found her, sir. Back of the boat. Reading under a blanket. Fits your description. Asked her for her ID; said we're running a security exercise. She didn't quibble. Want me to ask her to come see you?'

Security exercise. The words jarred for Drew. Even his second in command had no idea of the extent of the security issues he and the ship currently faced. It was unprecedented and highly confidential. Multiple frauds and thefts at sea with a pattern that suggested this was organised criminal activity. And he'd never once in his career had his staff and passengers as under the microscope at they were this trip, to the point that there were security specialists and police on board. And that didn't sit well with a man who was meticulous about 'tight ship'. It caused something bad to curl inside his gut.

'Good work, Hale. And no, just checking on her safety.' The lengths he'd gone to were perplexing on every level. Drew felt his stomach relax now that he knew she was well, outside on deck. Not ill, just choosing to no-go-zone him again. 'Thanks. Appreciated.'

'Anything else, Captain?'

'No. She's just an old friend of the family.' Why was he explaining, anyway?

Drew knew usually he'd pass a request to check on a passenger to one of his liaison team members. But after he'd scanned dinner tables without success, he'd called a search. She'd been quiet and withdrawn throughout their time together in his office. Given little away; clammed up and let Edna Randall talk. She'd still held his interest captive, however.

The light breeze and clear stars created the perfect night for a walk on deck. On his way he checked at the helm to make sure all was in order with his officers on watch. Five minutes more and he found her, alone. She appeared so young in her striped cotton sweater and cotton twill preppy trousers.

Libby Grant sat huddled in a blanket, her feet curled under her like a child, reading. The scene made his lips twitch into a smile. She'd used to look just like that — bookworm and beautiful — and his heartbeat still upped tempo. Her brown hair had curled in the breeze and sea air. He found he liked it better that way.

'Libby. You feeling better now?' he asked softly.

She looked up so sharply and with such a gasp of shock it made him step back. Her e-reader gadget slipped and bounced onto her chair then crash-landed on deck with a smack. The dismay on her face rocked him especially because he noticed that her hands shook.

'You scared me,' she admitted.

'I'm sorry. I didn't mean to startle you.'

'Our jinx returns.' She stood, looking down at the smashed gadget at her feet.

'There was no jinx. Just bad timing. Like now,' he parried.

Her gaze flicked back to his. 'You often creep up on passengers in the dark?'

It rankled him that she accused rather than accepting his apology. 'I was concerned you weren't well.'

'I'm fine. No need to worry on my account.' Her answer was definitely curt. And it reminded him of his own attitude in his earlier security meeting, when again his staff had been under scrutiny about instances of theft on board. He liked to think his crew were all above board in the honesty stakes. A cruise ship was a family — a big one, admittedly, but still one of the most tight-knit of workforces there were.

Her dismay at him nailed him, especially when Drew saw her reading gadget smashed on the deck. He knew he'd go right back to search in his cabin, to dig out that book gadget thing he'd never used. He could send one of his officers to deliver it to her. Just being nice. Passenger satisfaction only. Nothing more in it at all.

'Alone on this trip?' He'd itched to ask her earlier but hadn't got a chance.

'My aunt planned this special trip, but she passed earlier this year. Decided I'd still do it in her honour. Going solo felt scary, but it's proved to be fine. But I've already made friends,' Libby confided. 'I'm relaxing and finding my groove.'

'I'm sorry for your loss.'

Was there anything he could do or say right around Libby? He should have learned to leave well alone long ago. He might have the skills to sail a boat through tricky tides and tight spaces — but Libby was still the woman who'd never let him in. He'd always found her mesmerising, but she'd been too busy chasing her dreams of perfection, in love and career both. He'd never stood a chance with her career and her dreams. And her dashed esteem. Libby had always been out of his reach.

And Drew now knew there was no such thing as perfect. There was grabbing life. Because every day counted. And perhaps your time might be cut shorter than you realised. He'd found a piece of rare treasure he'd forgotten about today. And it still shone bright when rediscovered. It just had little desire to re-engage with him.

'Sorry. I can sense I'm intruding here. I'll leave you in peace,' he said, turning away. He wondered why he'd bothered to find her in the first place. He had enough trouble and disappointment on his shoulders on this voyage without more; he might just have a career to salvage soon. As if he hadn't enough of a share of heartache in recent years.

'Don't go, Drew! I'm sorry for being snappy.'

Her voice whirled him back round, and the surprise in his expression was clear. Libby knew Drew didn't realise how much he took her breath away. Not just the uniform, but the job. And the way he looked right at her as if he saw what lay inside her heart.

There were now laughter lines around his eyes, and slight greying at his temples. Plus a complexion that told her he made use of his shore leave in foreign climes.

'Can we start over?' she asked so softly she barely heard it herself. But she had to face up to what she needed to say.

'You think we can?' he asked.

'I'd like to. Sit beside me. Please — I have things to say to you.'

'Let me clear up the mess I made first,' he offered.

'Leave it for now,' she told him. He approached and she kept her gaze fully latched onto his. 'I think it's me who should be saying that to you. I made a mess. So I should be apologising — which is part of the problem here.'

A pause hung heavy between them and still she kept her gaze steady. She'd needed to make peace, clear up the misunderstandings and admit she'd been wrong. Edna Randall had been right all along.

'I'm sorry for the way I acted in the past,' she admitted, hugging her sides.

'It's okay.' He dismissed her with a hand.

Libby shook her head. 'Not to me it isn't.' She was glad to have the feelings finally out into the open. As a lawyer, justice drove her in all things. And here was the man who of all people was entitled to feel ill done to by her. She owed him his due. She'd left a note, walked away. She'd bypassed his right of appeal.

'I should never have ended things that way. I've wanted to admit that for a very long time. When I met you today, I was trying to escape because of embarrassment and guilt.'

'I'm grateful for the confessions. But honestly, water under the bridge. That was a long time ago now,' he confided. 'There's no need for you to feel so bad about this. I forgive you. We all do foolish things when we're young.'

His smile melted her reserve. He'd said he forgave her. She really hoped he could.

'I got your note to say you couldn't make dinner tonight. I thought I'd check you're okay,' he explained.

'I'd planned a light meal.'

'Let me pick this up now.' Drew hunkered down and retrieved and placed the flat-lined e-reader on the end of a nearby steamer chair. 'It doesn't look fixable.'

'At one time I'd have said that about a truce between us, but we're managing,' she told him. Then added, 'I didn't bring books with me.'

'We have a ship's store. I'll reimburse — '

'It'll make me active if I don't keep reading all the time. I'm already a regular at 'deck boules for beginners'.'

'Must check the schedule and drop by.' He laughed, which was good. Laughter might not heal past hurts, but it certainly soothed them.

'If you've other places to be, don't let me keep you,' she added. 'I just hope we can let the past stay in the past and maybe still be friends again? I was emotionally immature when we split. I liked you a lot — I honestly just felt like a failure for messing up.'

'You're kidding, right?'

Libby blew out a breath. 'I thought I wasn't the kind of girlfriend you needed back then. I thought I was too clumsy, geeky and boring. But I should have been decent and talked about it first.'

'So why the frostiness earlier?' he asked her, and Libby felt a rush of discomfort that he'd clocked it when she'd thought she'd covered up.

'Plain old guilt. I hope you didn't think it was a slight, me not eating with you. I was trying to make it easier on both of us.'

'I invited you because I wanted to. Not out of politeness.' Drew closed the space between them and reached out to take her hands in his. His touch was warm and soothing, and her heart beat a fast tattoo in her chest. And while it surprised her completely, Libby swiftly went with the feelings that had been bubbling inside her since she'd locked eyes with him. It felt amazing, like old times. 'I don't have any issues about our past. Well okay, I was hurt and disappointed, but not anymore. I'm your captain. And I want you to have the cruise of a lifetime. I don't want 'us' getting in the way of that. From here on in, your vacation is what counts.'

He smiled at her so hard Libby had to gulp back the rush of disappointment she'd felt. He was doing his job. What had she been hoping for? Promises? Rekindled romance? Feeling mortified, Libby pulled herself swiftly together, then felt a fool. 'I intend to do everything I can to achieve that, Captain Muldoon.'

'Please call me Drew. Then we're both in accord,' he answered. 'I'd like to catch up. Maybe lunch when I'm not on captain's-table duty. Grab a light bite? The grill café does a mean wrap or a salad.'

She watched him stare out to a dark inky sea. So unaltered and yet so changed. In looks he was Drew, but better. She wondered what the years had done to rub away his bright energy and enthusiasm for life. Was it responsibility?

'We dock in Malaga tomorrow. You planning on sight-seeing?'

'I've dreamed of this trip. Travel and immersing in other worlds.'

'There'll be amazing sights. Cartagena, Ibiza, then Barcelona. It's one of my favourite cities. Then Monte Carlo, and Portofino. Pisa and Rome.'

Libby couldn't suppress her excitement at adventures ahead. 'I love all of it, but Italy is the part I'm desperate about. I love cooking and Italian food. I'm pretty keen to see Barcelona too.'

Drew smiled. 'You won't be disappointed. I was serious about lunch. Fancy it?'

Libby shook as the sea currents made a breeze whip up. 'Let's see how things go.' A strong cold breeze suddenly left them both blown and shivering. 'Nice to see you again. Sorry about the awkward bridge tour.'

'It's great to see you again,' he concluded and moved away. He began to walk off before he turned and added, 'No more hiding from me in future? You can get past mistakes if you try hard enough,' he told her.

And as much as the words struck her, she also couldn't get past the fact that he'd become more charming than he'd been at twenty-three.

'Goodnight Captain Muldoon. Try not to cause more catastrophes.' She threw her broken e-reader in a nearby bin, then walked away in the opposite direction.

'Stay safe, Libby Grant — if possible,' he called after her.

Libby walked faster, realising she'd gone the wrong way. She was in over her head already, and not just with directions — with the charms of a man who always caused her turmoil at every turn.

⋆ ⋆ ⋆

'Good morning. This is your captain. I trust you're enjoying your voyage. Please mark your calendars for a formal dinner this Friday. We've just docked in sunny Malaga on a glorious day, and I hope you enjoy your visit.'

The announcement made Libby stop in the middle of sipping her coffee.

She'd been hoping the espresso would kick her brain into ready life. But Drew's voice acted faster, especially when she could read 'ensnared' in the wistful looks of female passengers sitting nearby witnessing his PA announcement. Clearly he was the ship's hottest catch.

She sighed; last night she'd had a dull awareness that the signs of hidden chemistry lingered, but she was scared to acknowledge it lest she was imagining it. And maybe it was all hankering on her part only. And her pathetic foot-in-mouth tendencies around Drew had not improved. They were worse.

'Goodnight, Captain Muldoon. Try not to cause any more catastrophes.' Saying that to the man in charge of a passenger liner! She'd walked off and ended up at the nude bathing passengers' area (she'd seen the signs). He must have known where she'd gone.

She replaced her cup in its saucer, splashing the hot dark coffee on her linen shorts, like a hot danger sign to leave the past where it belonged.

'Libby! Libby! Look who we've brought.' Edna Randall's voice intimated more chaos about to land. She sported a lurid tangerine-orange jumpsuit and matching headband today. 'Silly girl. You've messed up your clothes. You'll keep the ship's laundry room busy. You and your accidents. Always getting into a scrape or two.' She turned to the woman beside her, intimating that her speech had been by way of introduction. 'Libby's lovely when you get past her clumsy ways. Lucky for her we're on hand to help.'

The smiling woman accompanying Edna was perfection personified with a bright smile. She was well-groomed in a scarlet pencil skirt and beige company livery jacket, and matching shade of lipstick. Her slick bun clinched the best-hairstyle award, and her legs were showstoppers on stilettos.

'Thanks, Edna,' said Libby. 'Hi. Nice to meet you.' Libby stuck out a hand in greeting.

The woman smiled. 'Hi. I'm Sienna Hudson, ship's dancer. I'm here seeking a favour. We're under pressure today and Edna's told me your secrets.'

Libby dared to think. 'What rumours are you circulating, Mrs Randall?'

'Your spin-cycling hobby makes you useful, but more of that later.' Edna pushed her ever-low-sliding spectacles back to where they should sit and took in a breath. 'Sienna dances like a dream, Libby; you two should get acquainted. I 'volunteer engineered' you in to help her today.'

'What am I doing now?' Libby asked, wishing Edna would resist the intervention.

But Edna wasn't ready to finish her lecture. 'Next time you'll catch Sienna's shows. Where do you hide out at nights anyway? If you spend your time aboard with your nose in a book, you'll miss the highlights, and that would be a shame.'

Libby forced her smile to stay. 'What's she said I'll do?'

'I understand from your friends you spin-cycle every week. Today we're having an aqua spin challenge in the main-deck pool. I badly need helpers, and it's for a very good cause. A charity event; you'd be getting me out of a tight spot.'

Was nothing she'd told the Randalls in casual mid-dinner conversation off limits? Yes, she spin-cycled. She also did body combat and sometimes Pilates. She hadn't banked on her hobby list having public scrutiny. 'What's the cause?'

'Cancer Answers. It's a charity that helps support patients after diagnosis. Today's a day of concerted charity fund-raising — kicking off with aqua spin to music, and the staff have been challenged to be involved all day. We do an hour's nonstop spin-cycle class in the main-deck pool while volunteers rattle buckets for donations. The passengers request the music, and it's great cardio. But my dancer friend rolled his ankle yesterday and another has a tummy bug. We had new passengers arrive today, and first-day passengers have the fullest wallets. Sound doable?'

'How could I refuse?' Libby nodded. 'Cancer is a cause I like to support on a personal level, so I'll help, though I'm not saying I'll have the stamina. Count me in.'

'Hard selling, aren't I? But I'll owe you a favour back.' Sienna bit her lip. 'I'm on good terms with the spa girls. Does a treatment on me sound like a payback deal?'

Libby grinned. 'Actually, I can think of a better idea. Your pointers for the best port excursions and must-see places when we dock? Nothing beats seasoned expertise.'

Sienna grinned back. 'You're on. I'd love to help.'

Libby lowered her voice while Edna was otherwise engaged ordering from the coffee bar, but nodded slightly towards her. 'If I'm honest, I could do with an escape. Edna's lovely, but too firm and strict for vacation relaxation.''

Sienna giggled. 'I think we can both help each other on this trip. You should hang out with us. Come and find me at the Starlight Stage or message me at the desk.' She handed Libby a card with her details on. 'Rehearsals and shows every day except Monday and Thursday.'

If nothing else, the event would offer a respite. And it was for charity; her godmother had lost her fight with cancer, so this was a personal cause. Plus the exercise could be useful. She could splurge at tonight's buffet in good conscience.

She answered, 'I'm in. A good deed is never wasted.'

Sienna remarked, 'Should I have mentioned there's an outfit?'

Libby closed her eyes. 'Why am I starting to think I may regret this?'

'A sash with shorts and a T-shirt. And afterwards we usually shake buckets and tour the ship offering hugs for cash. Kisses if you're brave. You'll rock the look, by the way. I'll even let you pick off hunky guys, since I'm just back off honeymoon.'

Libby had to laugh. Despite the impromptu involvement, she already liked Sienna. She sensed an exuberance that was catching. 'I'll never knowingly turn down a hug with a hunk.'

The women laughed. 'Great,' Sienna said. 'See you at the main-deck pool, twenty to four sharp. Cancer Answers is set to make money this trip.'

Edna stared at Libby with her hands on her tangerine-suited hips. 'Figured you needed young company.' She winked at Libby. 'Not as evil as you think, huh?'

Libby stared back. 'Edna, please stop taking over my life. I mean that in the nicest, most diplomatic of ways. From this moment onwards you're not railroading me. Got it?'

Edna stared then slowly blinked. And for an awful moment Libby realised her 'putting it out there' firm approach might backfire. Then Edna threw her head back and cackled. 'Wondered how long it would take to get stroppy. I like your ballsy side; I'm only making you step outside your limits for your own good.'

Walt appeared beside her. Today he wore another Cruise Company baseball hat, this time in a tangerine hue. 'Leave the girl, Edna. She knows law, and I'm pretty sure you're breaking some.'

Edna pushed his arm. 'I'm only looking out for her.'

Libby retorted, 'I'm keeping a list for when karma strikes her back.'

3

'Now aren't you glad I press-ganged you to say yes?' said Sienna, smiling like she'd just been proven right and got the trophy for it.

'You're lucky I'm in a good mood after my first excursion to Malaga,' Libby answered.

'Enjoy it?' Sienna's smile dazzled almost as much as the fascinating trip Libby was still bursting with.

Libby couldn't contain her excitement. 'Definitely. Had a guided tour of Malaga Cathedral, then a tapas tasting. Strolled the plazas, browsed boutiques, and the sweet *tarta Malagueña* with coffee was delicious.'

'Wow. You crammed the highlights in.'

'I loved the painted walls and symbols that told the truth about past conquests of the city by Christian troops. The Mercado Atarazanas was a highlight; its sights and smells had me salivating. I finished with Plaza de la Constitución and Calle Larios.' She smiled. 'I'm warming to cruise life; I'm excited about Cartagena now. I can't wait for more local gastro specialities.' She put her fingers to her lips and kissed them.

Sienna grinned. 'This challenge will work off the treats. That outfit suits you too.'

Libby regarded her reflection. 'You lied.' She took in the tiara and feather boa. 'It's way more O.T.T. than you let on. If my work colleagues saw me, I'd never hear the end of it. Nowhere to hide.'

'You have pins worth revealing.'

'Says the woman with legs up to her armpits.'

For Libby this was the definition of moving out of her comfort constraints. David would have told her to change immediately. Seriousness was his watch-word; being a law partner to him meant seriousness and life limitations. She'd vowed she was going to change her life and expand her horizons. She guessed this was rebellion supreme.

'I can take a pic?' Sienna pushed. 'Anybody ever tell you that your eyes dance when you're annoyed?'

The ship's captain once did. Remembering that made her blush. Libby threw her feather boa over her shoulder. She now had a glimpse of what life as an ocean liner's dance troupe member must be like.

They went out on the busy, noisy deck where music already pumped, and walked through the passengers watching and waving at their charity-dress splendour. It was hard to stay mad when the antics caused open smiles. When they reached the pool, Libby saw the rows of metal spin bikes placed in the shallowest end.

'Done aqua spin before?' Sienna checked.

'No. Just normal spin-cycling. But I can swim.'

'The water gives more resistance. Pretty gruelling, but once the music starts it's hard not to get caught up in the fun. Fabio the instructor pushes hard, be warned. They do sit-ups on the bike seats and some arm-resistance exercises. Be prepared.'

'Now she tells me,' Libby muttered, then winked.

'Fancy a date tonight?' a young male onlooker shouted down.

'I don't think she'll be able to take on much later,' Sienna answered back. 'But make a big enough donation and anything's possible.'

The guy smirked and a friend high-fived him. Another four similarly dressed women came to descend into the pool, each leggy and lithe and either dancers or instructors. They all waded into the water as more and more passengers crowded around the pool's periphery. Some officers and ship's personnel appeared with buckets for cash, and many called down with encouragements.

The nearby DJ cranked up some music as Libby found her bike and made some adjustments to the tension.

'Give it all you've got, Lib. Don't flag,' said Sienna, only then waving dramatically at a swarthy officer standing nearby the pool's railings. Libby recognised him as the one who'd security checked her on the deck last night. 'That's my gorgeous husband. So cute. I marvel at how lucky I am.'

The officer threw his wife a wink. 'Show us what you're made of.'

Sienna confided, 'Seeing him in his uniform still gives me crush jitters.'

But there was no more time for chatting as a muscular instructor in tight cycling shorts and a racer vest climbed into the pool wearing shades and mounted his bike at the front of the pool. He needed no introduction, primarily because his top had 'Fabio' emblazoned across his sculpted chest. The party vibe quickly took hold as Fabio crowd-roused. His microphone headset enabled him to turn the event into a performance.

Libby and the rest of the crew were soon involved in a warm-up. She was too busy getting set to worry about her appearance. That she was in shorts and T-shirt and a boa, looking like a crazy person, only then realising that there was a guy on board she really didn't want to happen upon her. She mentally crossed fingers that Drew was too busy sailing the ship.

She forced Drew's image from her thoughts, then made a silent prayer of, 'Don't let him see me. Get this over with quickly.'

★ ★ ★

Drew's morning had brought serious issues to occupy him. He'd had no spare time to consider the amazing events of the night before and Libby's stark apology and confessions. Mainly because in all his career, he'd never had the company's crime wing working on board; but this trip brought fresh challenge and their obligatory support.

Prior concerns had been raised regarding theft. It caused question marks because it was small amounts across the ship's services and some passenger accounts. So far no culprit had been identified or apprehended. CCTV footage had so far yielded nothing. Drew didn't want to consider that there could be a criminal element in his staff, but all avenues had to be pursued. And after all, there were 800 staff to supervise in total. But the meeting had brought stark wake-up calls that unsettled him; it was now evident that fraud and theft were continuing on this voyage, which meant a staff cause was likely and suspected. The development jarred. Security officials were ruling out a passenger culprit at this stage.

He tried to push his concerns away for the moment and took his usual 'walk the floor' promenade on deck. He'd seen Libby head off with the excursion group to Malaga, Picasso's birthplace. It was a shame he was so tied up, since he knew the best places to visit in the port; but work took top priority.

Now Drew wondered if all the excursion passengers were back. Given strict schedules and rules on punctuality in vacating port, they'd learn the hard way if not. As he approached the main pool area, pulsing dance music filled the air. The volume increased, and he remembered today was the Cancer Answers fundraiser push. A cheering crowd swelled and he lingered to absorb the atmosphere, lured on by the sight of his master sommelier Jackson, who rarely appeared beyond the dining room or cellar.

'Hey Jackson, great to see you.'

'Likewise, Captain. Lots of happy faces today.'

It was only then that Drew's brain engaged, realising that Jackson too wore the teal Cancer Answers sash over his uniform.

'Your support is appreciated.'

Drew's partner Josie had begun the charity to raise awareness of her ovarian cancer. She'd started fundraising after giving up shipboard work. The effort had helped her cope with treatment and gave her a fresh direction. Jackson had trained her from junior to top of her game as head of food and dining, but chemo visits hadn't been practical with ship work. This year Cancer Answers had grown in stature and was his nominated captain's charity again. Drew put a great deal of time into planning Josie's legacy.

'How's the collection going?' he asked.

'Already enrolled several passengers for ongoing monthly donations, and sold tickets for the charity dance,' Jackson answered. He held out a three-quarters-full bucket stuffed with money.

'Fantastic. Josie would have been in there yelling her head off.' Drew felt his gut clench even as he mentioned her, and inside him something speared at the mixed emotions. They'd met through work. She'd been one of the most exacting women he'd ever met or indeed worked with, and she'd lived for her job. Her passing had changed him, not always for the better. 'We don't see each other often enough, do we, Jackson?'

'Drop by the wine store, or invite me up to the bridge.'

'I'll do that. Though hiding out with you in the wine store sounds like the better option.'

'Always welcome, Drew.' The slip to his name was intentional because the men were long-time friends.

As the music track changed, Drew turned back to the pool. The cinema screen above featured the pool's participants, likely being filmed by the ship's on board Cruise Channel TV crew. He joined in the hand-clapping himself until a familiar face snagged his attention and made him stop. Libby, in jazzy charity clothing, smiled as she worked out at full tilt. With earnest determination.

'Captain. Great to see you again,' said a voice nearby. 'Surprised you aren't in the water showing us what you're made of. You look like a man who takes fitness seriously.' Edna Randall sported a lemon sun visor, shorts and a vest.

'I had other duties.'

She reached out to pat his shoulder. 'I think you'd be outstanding in action.'

He looked back at the screen, wishing the camera hadn't left Libby so he could continue to watch.

Edna rebuked, 'You should wear shorts, Captain Muldoon. Don't captains have shorts in their uniforms these days?'

'Are you always this flirty with my staff, Mrs Randall?'

She laughed. 'Speaking of flirtation ... our Libby's doing a great job fundraising. She fills out shorts very nicely.' Edna nodded to the shallow-end action. She must have seen his gaze return there. The screen again flashed to her as she worked out, rising and falling in time with the instructions ordered her way.

'And how did she get recruited?'

'Helpful as well as generous. Spin-cycling's her thing. It was me who volunteered her. You interested in our girl, Captain? She's something of a feast for the eyes today . . .'

The screen flashed a much-splashed picture of the object of their conversation laughing and soaked, her T-shirt plastered to her repeat-look inciting form. Drew felt his face heat as Edna regarded him intently.

'And she's a favourite with the men folk,' Edna added.

A throng of chanting male fans had Drew's stomach go free fall. His interest was piqued, but irritation burned. He stared at the assorted members of his crew all furiously cycling on their spin bikes as directed by Fabio, who ordered them to be faster and better, and they all took things as seriously as if they were powering the mighty ship's engines. The sound of money rattling in buckets added to the mayhem.

Drew noticed he was holding his breath, and his heartbeat had upped tempo. 'You didn't answer my question, Mrs. Randall. This is a crew event. I'm surprised to see a passenger involved.' Not to mention that the liability if she were hurt was more than he wanted to contemplate.

'The lovely Sienna needed volunteers to sub for downed crew. She's great company when she stops worrying about the calories of the buffet. And I think you should thank her for being quick to help. Maybe offer a drink?'

'I was planning to issue a lunch invitation. We're old friends,' he said, starting to feel Edna Randall must have lessons in espionage and manipulation.

'I think I'd gathered that much. Not that she'd told me. Thanks for the intel, Captain,' Edna said from behind a hooded gaze. 'Just make sure you ask her out until she accepts.'

'Two, four, six, eight. Everybody clap your hands to encourage the crew,' ordered Fabio loudly over the PA system in a heavy accent. 'Let's take this to the next level. Faster!'

Drew wasn't taking notice of Edna Randall anymore. Only Libby commanded his attention. The bronzed skin, a tiara bobbing as she rose up and down in steady moves to the music. Her limbs shaking at the intensity. But she coped like a swan above the swell. A count of eight standing cycled beats. Then a count of eight seated. Then the pace increased. And still Libby kept up with smooth ease as if she did this kind of crazy caper all the time.

She took his breath away. Nailed his attention. And coherent words to reply to Edna failed to form. 'She's a good egg,' he found himself saying. Like an idiot.

'You didn't think the helm tour showed her to best advantage? That girl hides her light under a bushel. You'd do well to remember that.'

What was Edna up to? And what was Libby made of, iron? Some of the dancers had flagged, especially now that Fabio urged his small troupe to sit on their cycle seats and do sit-ups to the same punishing rhythm. Libby was fit. Libby made a mark in whatever she did. Libby made him tongue-tied. And she was in his ship's pool raising money for a charity the woman he'd once loved had founded. Raw emotions surged inside him that made his jaw ache, and Drew itched to leave.

The event crescendo came with a punishing fastest-pace conclusion that ended with wild clapping and applause. Drew found himself watching intently as Libby was hugged by her dancer comrades. He stood, wanting to go, then not wanting to miss saying thanks.

As the wet conquerors climbed from the pool, Edna shouted, 'You crazy girls. Don't drip all over us — keep back!'

Libby neared, and Drew saw her

falter by the way her eyes left his. She shrugged, pulled away stuck-tight clothes, and shook her boa.

'Nice work, Libs,' said Edna, unknowingly mimicking his one-time private nickname for her.

Libby answered, 'You deserve a soaking for putting me in the deep end, Edna Randall.' But she was joking. She stood beside Drew with her accomplice Sienna, dripping wet and shivering despite the hot day.

Meanwhile Drew tried hard not to notice her legs and the shorts that could stop traffic. Her hair was wet-streaked mayhem in a messy bun. 'Well done,' he told them. 'It was kind of you to step in.' His pulse went crazy when her gaze flicked his way. 'Thanks for supporting my charity.'

Sienna butted in, 'The captain's nominated charity, Cancer Answers. We've been aiming for half a million euros. We're already in sight of target.' She looped her arms around Libby's neck as the ship's photographer took a photo, then rattled off more camera shots of the group *en masse.*

'Duty calls. Keep up the sterling effort.' Drew stepped from their orbit. He needed to go. He'd already seen the chalkboard poster advertising hugs for cash with the pool participants. Did he really want to witness that? No; but just as he turned, he overheard Sienna's conversation.

'Let's go and squeeze hunks for cash. What a job.'

'Hey, you're married,' Libby answered.

Sienna added, 'Don't tell Hale. Anyway, no one else can compete with his hugs.'

Drew departed from the main passenger deck. Retreating to the operation lair was way preferable to flirty spontaneity with euphoric women in a party mood. But as he strode away, he knew Edna watched him. These women were worth avoiding. And maybe they'd jointly just set him up for tactical temptation without his consent.

★ ★ ★

Hale chilled in the officers' lounge, yet he'd just caused Drew fifty fathoms of challenge. Drew had found the officer, previously known as his best friend, in his favourite hideout. 'You're in a whole lot of trouble,' he stated and closed the door hard. He vowed to make sure he created awkward rosters in future as revenge. It might even cause some complaints from his new wife, which would serve him right. 'Before you say a single word, I know it was you. It has Sienna's meddling written all over this. Tell her she needs to keep out of my business.'

'What are you talking about?' Hale kept his attention fixed on the print before him.

'She knows not who or what she meddles with.'

Hale looked up from his newspaper and regarded his boss with narrowed eyes. 'What do you mean?'

'Somebody set me up to see a

passenger at a disadvantage. Somebody befriended her on purpose. Any ideas?'

Hale sighed. 'What am I supposed to have done?'

'Your wife has made a new friend on purpose. Were you in on this together?' Drew felt his jaw tighten. The urge to send his friend's newspaper behind the sofa made his fingers twitch. He wished he hadn't asked for help finding Libby on deck that night. Also wished he'd kept the situation personally handled and the e-reader to himself too. And now he had that image branded on his brain. Libby laughing and being applauded. In shorts and giving out hugs with pink-painted toenails in flip-flops. The thundering certainty that right now she was parading in that come-hither disarray, with men claiming hugs for money, had him fit to growl. So Hale could take the flack.

'Not guilty. And anyway, what's the problem?'

'You told Sienna. Sienna befriended her. And now I find your wife taking

Libby Grant under her wing. We know she's crazy for matchmaking. She's already caused all kinds of scrapes in the past, and I'd hoped she'd learned better.'

'Ever think you might be assuming too far? Any what's the issue? This has nothing to do with you, Drew. You're paranoid.' The look on Hale's face wound Drew up fit to blow brain springs. 'I can't be held responsible for Sienna. You know these ship's dancers. I only happened to mention the e-reader delivery when she asked where I'd been. She is entitled to know, now we share a cabin.'

'I'm not involved with Libby. We're old friends,' Drew protested.

'And my wife needs answers when somebody gets me out of bed to run his errands. There's always a price to pay for playing outside the rulebook . . . ' Hale cleared his throat. 'And maybe you should wake up and realise it is okay to move on.'

Drew processed the fact that he'd

lost the argument and forced himself to sit in the chair opposite his friend.

'Josie's gone, Drew. It's okay to be alive.' Hale shook his head. 'You may be hot on navigation, but you're taking a wrong turn if you think you can get through this trip telling yourself you're not into the lady who makes you act so out of character. It's on the horizon already.'

Drew sighed, defeated. 'It's all past tense. Emphasis on the tense.'

Hale folded his newspaper. 'I don't need sonar to read it a mile off that you're uptight about her. It's in the water. You'll hit it at some point.'

'The only thing I want hit is the off switch.'

'Do you really believe that?'

Drew watched him calmly walk out through the door. He scratched his jaw and sea-watched through the window, unable to raise any useful reply except, 'What did I do to deserve the lectures?'

4

Waiting in the line for entry to the dining room, Libby was consumed in thinking that earlier when she'd met Drew he'd seemed preoccupied and uptight. Maybe standing in during a crew-led charity event meant she'd overstepped and incurred his censure.

'We meet again — with perfect timing,' said an unfamiliar male voice nearby.

Libby turned to see who'd hailed her. The man had dark collar-length hair and a chiselled jawline, and he wore shades and a suit. Last time she'd seen him was during fund-raising when he'd worn shorts and a linen shirt with those shades on deck. He'd oozed effortless confidence, and she recognised him as his smile was his signature.

He continued, 'Meeting again so

soon must be destiny. Or my very good fortune.'

'Oh, right, we shared a charity hug. Thanks for your generous donation. The event went well, and we had great fun.'

'You often get tied up in all things extracurricular?' he asked. The man smiled in a flirty but not unwelcome way. He was no taller than Libby in her heels; in fact he was a little shorter. Unconventionally handsome, his face, topped with wavy dark hair, held character. He had a warm attractiveness. 'Would I be too forward if I offered to accompany you to dinner?' He mock-bowed. His accent was a mix of US with some UK pronunciations.

'As long as no more hugs are required. It's been a long day,' Libby warned. But a change of company might be welcome.

'Just your dazzling smiles,' he answered.

'How could I say no?' This man was an enigma that appealed to her curiosity.

Libby offered her hand. 'I'm Libby from London; a lawyer by profession. It's nice to meet someone new.'

'Zak Nazar, from California. Delighted to become your new dinner escort.'

Libby grinned at the über-obvious flattery. 'The food is delicious. It's resisting temptation that's the hard part.'

Zak removed and pocketed his shades and gave her an approving nod. His blue eyes twinkled. 'I endorse your appetites. What else are vacations for, if not to indulge the senses?'

The maître d' reached them and they were guided to a table quickly. Libby asked if Zak could join her at her usual allotted table. There was something familiar about this man that made her wonder at why his face tugged at her memory. She'd seen that face before, she was sure of it. Again his mysteries teased her. 'Your face is so familiar.'

He shrugged his shoulders. 'It's nice to meet someone who doesn't pounce. Fans usually ask me to take them on set or promise them a boxed set signed by the cast. I'm an actor; my current role is rather in vogue. We're famed worldwide. You likely saw a poster; I'm the lovable villain rogue. Hence the shades. It helps with crowd control.'

Libby put her hand to her mouth. 'I don't get much time for TV. Though now you've said it, I remember. You're hugely famous.' Libby grinned. 'Sorry. I know enough to say your show is fabulous. Why aren't you vacationing on a yacht away in private, if you don't mind me asking?'

'My role is why I'm on board. We're doing movie theatre showings with question sessions, and I'm giving on-set insights. It's a feature and a ticketed event. You must come. In fact, I'll insist it's in my rider.'

'Shouldn't you be eating in some VIP area?' Libby added. 'So you aren't deluged?'

Zak gave a wide smile. 'And miss out on all the best-looking dinner dates? I could be persuaded to private dining if you agree to join me.'

'Zak. I'm an anti-man zone. Trust me, this cruise is about me celebrating being single. I've only recently broken free.'

'Drat,' he answered. 'Shall we go and attack the buffet together?'

Libby nodded, and they'd just risen to move when a voice cried out nearby.

'Libby Grant. Of all the people to escape with!'

Clearly Edna had seen Zak's show and was a fan.

Libby whispered for Zak's benefit, 'I have to warn you, I have some shipboard friends. One means well but she's a little bold. She'll accost you whether you like it or not.'

'Worry not — I'm good at jousting. Let me rescue you from the dragon's lair.'

Libby stifled a giggle as Edna went into raptures over Zak. She realised maybe he was exactly what she'd needed: an anti-Edna threat disabling device with a sense of humour and plenty of charm and wit. They took Edna to the buffet, ready to change Zak's onboard life forever.

'Don't say I didn't warn you,' Libby said.

Zak answered, 'I intend to hold this against you for a long time. Favours will be owed. And I'll enjoy seeking out repayment.'

★　★　★

Drew toured the ship, a spring in his step and conviction in his heart. He'd find Libby and invite her to brunch and then a captain's dinner. Ask her outright if she had a partner or was seeing anyone. He couldn't believe he'd been so tardy and lacking in sense.

Maybe there was a shard of truth in what Hale had said. His feelings for Libby did linger. He might just need to confront the past. Friendship would be good as a first step. Romance need not be in the picture in the initial stages, but he didn't rule it out either.

Some last stragglers remained in the dining room. And Edna Randall proved easy to spot at her table with her husband, mostly due to her taste in bright colours. Tonight's ensemble was neon yellow worn with a matching hair feathery thing that looked like some exotic bird had lost plumage on her.

Drew strode towards her, seeing that Libby was absent but knowing that Edna would have full co-ordinates on her whereabouts, motivations and plans. He felt sorry for Libby's plight. She deserved better than on-board badgering.

'Captain. So gratifying that you pay us so much individual attention.' Edna rose to grab his arm with a fierce grip. 'Will you dance?'

'I'm afraid not, Mrs. Randall. Great to see you again. Pleasant dinner, I trust?'

'Delightful. We've found a star acquaintance. He's taken a shine to our girl.'

Drew stood to full height as something constricted inside him. His good mood bottomed as he felt wrong-footed. He raised his eyebrows to encourage further explanation. 'And who would that be?' No doubt Edna would ably oblige. Heavens, but the woman loved to talk.

'She's dancing with him.' Edna gestured towards the dance floor in the distance. 'He challenged her that he'd pay good money to Cancer Answers if she joined him for a tango. He's quite a character; and such a coup that you have him on board.'

Realisation dawned. The resident film star he'd met earlier was now Libby's current companion. 'Zak Nazar?' he answered. 'Yes. We're very privileged.'

'They're in the Neptune Starlight Ballroom together.'

Drew wished he'd got to her first. 'Could you pass on I'd like to talk with her? A brief word. Perhaps she can get front of house to call me?'

'Certainly, Captain.' Edna smiled.

The twinkle in her eye gave away her keen intelligence. 'Once her dancing feet stop, I'm sure she'll answer. What a busy girl our Libby is. The woman of the moment, no less.'

'Glad she's having an enjoyable cruise. You're ensuring her itinerary is packed.'

Drew bowed gracefully, talking to several tables of diners and barely registering a single word they'd told him, such was his preoccupation. He'd waited. And now another guy had jumped line. He strode to the ballroom, feeling his gut clench as he anticipated spotting them together.

'Evening, Captain,' said a female voice nearby. Nuala Delaney, the on-board excursions director, made no secret of her admiration. He'd always kept his distance as a result. 'Not often we see you down here unless it's formal night.'

Drew shrugged. 'Looking for a friend.'

'Interesting.' Her smile told him he'd

likely be discussed at length. 'We've been watching Zak, the guy who plays Troydon from *Great Players*. He really should be on *Dancing with the Stars*. Come see?'

He followed Nuala inside the ballroom and didn't need directing to the pair of them on the dance floor's centre. It was exactly as he had feared. Zak spun Libby in her lemon-yellow summer dress nipped in at the waist and so full in the skirt it whirled around her with a glimmer of sparkles; as did her hair, which was flying as she laughed at his antics. The guests sitting around the dance floor applauded each move. The swell of the swing band played the perfect backdrop to their show.

Her magic knew no end. Her expression and unbridled laughter told of carefree days. Her beauty speared him. A few days at sea and she'd found her mojo. And now she'd found a mentor. She'd got into her stride, but without him, never with him. And whenever he tried to intercept her, he was thwarted or too late. While she shone like a million meteorites.

'Catch you later.' Drew turned, not caring what Nuala thought of his reaction. He almost ran into a cocktail waiter holding a tray of glasses high, who saved the load with some effort and without complaint.

Nuala moved to follow him, but his body language must have made her realise his mood as she fell back. 'You okay, sir?'

'Due back on the bridge. See you around.' So much for charismatic captain.

Drew Muldoon really needed lessons in timing. And dancing. And putting women at ease, most specifically Libby. Because he craved her company and her sparkle.

She shone. Just not with him. He was beginning to realise he'd really lost her.

★　★　★

74

Libby sat waiting for Drew, her e-reader and blanket a cabin-retrieved shield for the occasion. She'd also grabbed a cotton jacket to cover her shoulders. Her lemon dress was dinner-pretty but was too thin for the deck's chill breezes.

She'd made an excuse of hurting her ankle; if Zak had recognised the lie, he didn't object. He'd vowed to sample cocktails and she'd opted to read in her cabin. But she'd gone to front of house after Edna had found her, with Drew's instruction. Trepidation tapped a rhythm in her stomach while she waited.

Drew rounded the corner, masterfully tall and so dashing in his officer's uniform, his stride full of purpose. What woman wouldn't swoon? But then that was at the root of all her Drew issues. He'd always been out of her league — the kind of guy women admired, and she'd never been able to keep up. She'd always been waiting for him to lose interest. In the end she'd got in first and saved him the bother. Why would hot stud Drew ever want a book nerd like her? How could she hope to keep him hers?

Pushing her spine straight, Libby plastered on a smile. 'Drew. You wanted me?'

'I do.'

She relaxed some. This could be okay. She just needed to keep calm and pretend he didn't suck away her ability to breathe. She had to stop behaving like a schoolgirl with her biggest crush. 'You on duty tonight?'

'I am.'

'And how's conditions?' Like she knew a dolphin's dictionary about cruise-liner sailing.

'Conditions are good. You're talking to me now, for one.' His gaze bored into hers.

'So why aren't you up there on action deck?'

'I have officers on watch. Don't worry, there's always somebody eagle-eyed. If you ever want to visit again, you only have to say. Spend a day up there, if you'd like to. I'm here because I want to talk to you.' He sat down on the steamer chair beside her. 'When are you going to get it into your head that I don't mistrust you in the least? And despite trying hard to get your attention, I never seem to succeed. I've been trying to talk to you properly and never managing to do so.'

She reared away from what he'd just confided. Confessions like that didn't help her control. And whenever she tried her hardest to impress Drew, it usually went wrong — which was why his mother had ended up with food poisoning, when Libby had cooked an important meal but had been so tied up in prepping a fancy dessert she'd totally forgotten vital things like defrosting properly and getting timings right.

The memory still curdled inside her: Drew's disappointed face as his mother was whisked away to be checked out by medics. As a result, she'd taken a culinary course and never looked back. She'd known Drew and his mother had a tricky relationship, and had hoped to excel. But instead she'd made it all unforgettably bad. She skidded away from memory lane.

'Did you enjoy dancing? You danced like nobody was watching, and I enjoyed witnessing it.'

She shrank back. 'You saw?'

'You're the talk of the ship,' he laughed. 'Is there no end to your talents? Cycling, dancing?'

She pushed his arm. 'Stop kidding me. Edna railroaded Sienna about the cycling. Zak forced me to dance. And Cancer Answers is the beneficiary.' She went into her purse, only then remembering, and handed over the 100 euros that Zak had given her for her wild dance moves bet. She might just be untangling hair knots for the rest of the night thanks to his spinning tactics.

Drew took the money and placed it in his top shirt pocket. 'Wow. He's very generous.' He stared at her hard and her breath caught. His citrusy shower-fresh cologne caused an ache inside her.

His gaze met hers. He still had that power; always had. And that was exactly what scared her most. She'd had her heart hurt so badly once before when she'd walked away from him, knowing it was for the best while breaking her apart.

'Can't believe we're skulking back here when you're the guy who runs the boat,' she whispered.

He shrugged his broad shoulders. 'You act like you don't feel comfortable around me.'

'I could say the same of you.'

Drew stared hard. 'Take my hand.' When she obliged, his thumbs brushed the backs of her knuckles. 'Are you involved, attached? I have to ask.'

Libby shook her head.

'I'm interested in getting to know you again, if you'll let me.' He sighed hard. 'Join me for lunch. I also want to invite you to join me at the captain's table. I want some time in private. We have a lot to catch up on, but I don't want to intrude on your vacation. And if Zak fancies you, it just shows he has good taste; and if you feel the same, I'll step aside. He's a catch — think of all the red-carpet parties you'd both go to together.'

Libby shook her head. 'He's not my type. Great fun. But romantically, no.'

Drew smiled then. 'Why am I pleased to hear that? So — lunch tomorrow?'

'I was planning a trip to Cartagena.'

'Brunch, then? Followed by dinner when I can get it arranged. And no, I don't often invite women to intimate special dinner dates.'

'Maybe you can give me tips for my trip to Catagena at brunch?'

He smiled. 'Happy to. It's a great place; lots of ambience. Ten o'clock at the Seacrest Grill. And I'll get back to you about dinner.'

Libby felt her heart zoom. That was euphoria, right there. And he'd caused it to light brightly inside her.

Drew reached out and squeezed her hand softly, and goose bumps immediately rose to life all over her skin's surface. Her pulse skittered while his gaze burned into hers.

'Sadly, I have to get back to the bridge now. Though I really don't want to.' He smiled. 'I'm looking forward to tomorrow already.' He leaned close and gently pulled her hand up to kiss it.

She grinned. 'Does that line usually work to make the girls weak at the knees? The bridge . . . me macho captain . . . you damsel seeking a sure place on the lifeboat.'

He threw his head back and laughed. 'I'd make sure you got in one even if you weren't speaking to me.' He grinned. 'You enjoying your time on board this luxury floating hotel?'

'It's living up to all my expectations.'

He paused for a beat. 'Can I ask . . . a guest is on vacation with his daughter and he's keen for her to pursue law as a career; would you give her the benefit of your experience? Usually the guests are asking me to talk about being a cruise captain.'

'Of course. Pass on my number and cabin room.'

'Her name is Lilly Lazlo. Her father is a long-standing cruise passenger with the company. And he's a big supporter of Cancer Answers.'

She stopped. There was a question she wanted to ask. 'Why did you pick a cancer charity? My godmother had breast cancer, so it's important to me on a personal level.' She'd wanted to ask Sienna but hadn't got a chance.

His regarded his shoes, then looked away. 'Lost my ex-partner that way. She passed on too fast. Ovarian cancer.'

Libby's face must have showed her shock, both at her own lack of insight and her probing innocence. 'I'm sorry, Drew. I'd no idea.'

'Many staff here knew her.' He cleared his throat, checked his watch then rose, and put out a hand to help her rise as well. But she was still in shock from the revelation.

'I apologise for intruding.'

'You didn't. You asked and I told you.'

They stood toe to toe. Libby felt her mind spin at Drew's stark impact on her physically. He made her breath catch and her heartbeat speed up.

'Skulking back here is no way to spend the vacation of your dreams. I suspect your celebrity suitor is a bit of a rogue who'd pull you in if he could. Especially if cocktails have emboldened his intentions. I'll escort you to your deck.'

Libby smiled as Drew led her on. 'I prefer a nice meal. Or a good book.' The touch of his fingers sent zinging sparks skittering through her. She couldn't remember it feeling so starkly affecting in her in her younger years when they'd held hands.

'Am I pushing boundaries?' he asked.

'I'm happy you are,' she whispered.

A smile tugged at the corner of his mouth, but hearing voices nearby, she stepped back. They approached a popular deck where a number of couples stood looking out to sea and others ambled arm in arm. Drew palmed his hair, and Libby couldn't quite believe how things had changed between them so swiftly. She blamed the romance of a luxury ship deck under starlight.

'Tomorrow is more promising than ever,' she whispered, making scary eye contact that made her quiver inside her high-heeled shoes. She walked beside him to the elevator.

He pressed the button and too soon it pinged, ready to take her to her cabin's floor. Libby noticed her disappointment at losing him. She didn't want to stop the conversation.

'Goodnight Libby. Sleep well,' he said.

She walked inside the elevator and willed herself not to trip or stumble even as the elevator doors closed. She'd spoken out, not kept her feelings tight, and she found she liked the freedom.

She suspected he'd sealed up his

heart. But something had made him want to open up tonight. Maybe it was her cue to be bolder too?

5

Libby's mouth opened in shock, then she stifled her laughter response. She nearly dropped her water glass, only saving it with a quick grab. She'd come to breakfast for an early coffee, saving her appetite for her brunch date.

But the sight of Zak Nazar striding to the breakfast buffet table in tasselled silk bedroom slippers and a dressing gown over pyjamas worn with dark shades was a shock to all who witnessed it. Had getting dressed been too much for him? His surly frown suggested as much. She dreaded to think what had ensued after she'd retired to her cabin. Ship's staff worked to lift their jaws from the floor as passengers watched and talked behind their hands.

Libby summoned composure as Zak flopped down beside her. 'Don't say a word. I can't bear your censure; I feel bad enough without a lecture.' Zak pulled in a laboured breath. 'My head is pounding like a marching drum band. Is it asking too much of you to have compassion?'

'You think you deserve any?' On a serious note, the man needed to sort his act out. Being a lawyer, she tried to give people the benefit of the doubt but also made sure they realised their judgement errors. 'Zak, you need to be mindful that the ship is your master, so you must adhere to rules. This ship is a 'family boat' rather than a 'party ship'.'

'Libby, can't you help me deal with this headache rather than make it worse?'

'I'm serious. Be mindful of your actions in future. You'll have to be prepared for consequences if you overstep.' She felt like a lecturing mother hen, but it did need to be said.

Zak let his head fell onto his hands. 'I need coffee; I couldn't even work out how to telephone for room service. Now there's a demolition crew in my head. I should have stayed and died alone and unloved in my cabin. You'd have found me eventually.'

'Not even funny. I've no reserves of pity when it's self-inflicted.' Libby poured the remains of her coffee pot into a cup and pressed it into his hand. 'You could be crossing lines that would sink your future. You're not at an after-filming party now.' Hollywood partying might not play well here. 'I'd suggest a big apology. What happened, anyway?'

'I'm an actor, darling girl; people expect a curtain call. And when I spark up a party, I do it at triple strength.' The only thing he appeared to need at triple strength right now was caution.

'I'd rather not represent you as a client by the time we dock. You could end up with a work ban.' She clinked her cup back in its saucer and he winced like she'd just thrown a grenade in his lap. Libby grinned behind a hand. Now half the dining room twittered around them.

Zak concluded, 'Next time you'll be my sobering influence and legal help, all rolled into one.'

Not if I can help it, thought Libby. 'Make sure you're safely in your cabin out of temptation's way in future.' She thanked the heavens she'd missed the shenanigans.

The waiter appeared with Zak's double-sized espresso, laid it down and scuttled back.

'A gallon more of coffee and some rest should fix my head.'

Afterwards Libby helped him from his seat, even though she'd never been more gawped at in her life. 'The excesses of a rogue celebrity,' she muttered. 'You definitely deserve the titanic migraine.'

⋆ ⋆ ⋆

After depositing Zak in his room, Libby returned to her cabin for her things. *En route*, she was accosted by a suited man and a teenaged girl who wore serious expressions.

'Libby Grant? I'm Carl Lazlo and this is my daughter Lilly. Captain Muldoon kindly told us you might speak with us. Are we imposing on your time?'

Recognition dawning, Libby shook his hand. 'Shall we walk out on deck to chat?'

The man agreed, and they went out to enjoy both the sunshine and the sight of the boat following the coastline on the way to the Cartagena port.

'My daughter is considering law as a study option for her degree.'

'Yes, Captain Muldoon told me.'

'Recently she's had second thoughts. I was hoping you might help answer some of her questions; reassure her. Changing her career choice now would have a big impact, and I think she could benefit from your advice.'

Libby let her gaze swiftly take in Lilly. She had long wavy brown hair and large eyes that an artist would leap to capture on canvas. Her body language told of a reserved nature and embarrassment at her current predicament. 'It's good to meet you, Lilly. You can ask me anything you want about my job. But how about we just meet later and I'll tell you about my working days in general?'

A smile gently tugged Lilly's mouth. 'Sounds great.'

'I don't mind answering any questions you have. I've worked in corporate law for ten years. I handle contracts for a large firm; it's exacting work, but it's also challenging, and it can be fun. I can run you through what my job entails and talk about the law studies part.'

'That'd be perfect,' said Carl. 'Doesn't that sound great, Lil?' He turned to his daughter, who was chewing on her lip but nodded eagerly, though Libby got a distinct feeling she'd rather talk maritime history.

Lilly shrugged her shoulders when her father caught her attention with his stare. 'Thank you, you're kind,' he said.

Libby got the distinct feeling she wasn't as at ease with things as her father hoped, so she decided she'd buy them both time. And making a new friend was no hardship. 'Why don't we meet later — say six o'clock? How about at the seats by the juice bar? That'll give you time to think up some questions and make some notes. Don't look so daunted. Your dad can stay or leave us and sit nearby for privacy — whatever he prefers. I promise it'll be painless.'

'That sounds perfect, Ms. Grant. She needs reassurance she's on the right track. Lilly's had doubts about her university place. We don't want her to blow her future,' Carl Lazlo added.

Again father and daughter exchanged looks, and Libby saw Lilly cast a glance at a passing teen boy who watched. Libby imagined she'd favour fun on this trip over career lectures. She hoped she could help, though she doubted her chances. She'd certainly give it her best shot.

★   ★   ★

Libby waited, seated in the on-deck grill at ten. She squeezed her excitement tight at the prospect. She'd enjoyed a peaceful hour after the Zak incident, reading crucial chapters of a newly started thriller that she could barely put down. All told, she was in a happy mood.

Bright sun bathed the polished deck, but the breeze brought enough chills to require covered shoulders. She'd donned a voile jacket over her capris and vest, figuring it said 'cool and casual'. She'd added sunshades to hide behind, which also meant she could scan for Drew's arrival.

She drummed her fingers and sipped from her glass of iced tea while strains of jazz music eased her nerves. Drew had been right about Zak; after his behaviour at breakfast she realised he was a time bomb. Though she thought he must have lurking reasons behind the drama-chasing. She also sensed he was a good, if misunderstood, guy at heart.

When Drew arrived, the picture of intense seriousness, she wondered what had caused the grey clouds in his mood. She rose when he arrived, out of courtesy.

'Drew. You okay?'

'Yes. Good to see you. Though I have a packed schedule today.' He shook his head but stopped to push back her seat in a gentlemanly fashion first. Then he sat opposite. 'I'm busy with pressing work issues, which is annoying, as it may mean I can't spare much time.' His answer was clipped. 'Apologies for my lateness. You slept well?'

'Very well. You do look stressed out today, Drew. Anything wrong?'

His jaw flexed. 'I'm afraid I have urgent meetings scheduled to start in thirty minutes, for which I apologise, but needs must.'

'I see.' Libby recognised the sharp twinge of disappointment that clawed inside her at his words. She'd so looked forward to this. And already the atmosphere from the night before had morphed into control and reserve. The spark had been doused. She'd been so looking forward to their date. She now wanted to build bridges and talk about the gaps that had grown between them. Yet he'd seemed keen before. Libby could only conclude he'd had second thoughts.

She forced a smile of acceptance. 'Look, you go and I'll eat solo. It's honestly not an issue,' she urged him.

Drew shook his head. 'No. I have some time. Have you ordered?'

'I waited for you first,' she admitted. And sadness tugged that he was clearly not in the frame of mind she'd hoped. Maybe the flirting was a figment of her hopeful imagination?

Drew summoned a waiter and they ordered swiftly.

'Work must come first,' she said

softly, meeting his gaze.

He told her, his tone lowered, 'I have something to ask you. I must suggest you keep away from Zak Nazar. I understand you've been taken in by his charms.' Drew stared at her, and Libby felt a knot inside her like an iron bar of doom. 'I understand you're a little too heavily involved with the man for your own good. But I thought I'd give you due warning that if he makes any more mistakes, he'll be left at the nearest port. His behaviour is reprehensible. Today we've had to tackle a clean-up operation thanks to his antics.'

'I walked him to his cabin this morning, if that's what you mean. I sat next to him at dinner, as we're both lone guests, but that's as far as we're connected. I danced with him for a charity donation.' Outrage simmered that she was even justifying herself. She'd done nothing wrong. And Zak's antics were completely his own doing and no reflection on her.

Their gazes sparked like flints. And

she couldn't douse her angry fire just because the one making the orders was the ship's first in command. 'Thanks for the concern, but it's my view that he's foolish and overzealous. I've given him firm words myself today. I don't tend to take kindly when people interfere with my choice of companion.'

Drew's gaze left her face and he sat straight, clearly displeased with her answer. 'Then I think you need to have a wake-up call about talking to him at all. I could disagree that you have a good handle on his measure. He is very much a danger, especially to other passengers on board and staff.'

Irritation ragged Libby at his high-handed, sweeping command-all judgements. Yes, she'd had a similar talk with Zak and given him her views, ones largely in accordance with Drew's. But his manner jarred with her sense of freedom. David had acted that way for way too long, and she'd only lately realised she'd been too meek. It had ultimately been a nail in the coffin of their future. And she'd vowed to never be talked down to again. She'd anticipated much better of Drew. He'd never acted this way in their prior relationship. But the years, and his position and shirt stripes, had changed him.

Just then the waiter came to serve them, and Libby's chargrilled veggie bruschetta looked amazing even though her appetite had vanished. Under other circumstances she'd have devoured it. Drew started on his omelette without further words exchanged. She was beginning to think their date hadn't just bombed, it had sunk without trace.

Libby narrowed her eyes. 'You go, and I'll see you some other time. When your mood is better.'

'Let's just eat, Libby.' She saw his jaw clench.

'I'm not sure I like the way you're judging me.'

He stared at her. 'Believe me, it's entirely for your own good.'

'You don't have the right to decree what I do.' Libby rose. 'Your only remit is the ship.'

David had been equally forceful; in such behaviours he'd excelled. He liked to be the arbiter of all that was 'appropriate'. Telling her what to wear. How to conduct her affairs and what he disapproved of. As her senior partner at work, she'd acquiesced — for too long: what to eat, what to read. It had become so oppressive that she'd known they had no future. He'd lived to control her life in minute regular detail.

But she was finally free. And she really hadn't expected a repeat. To feel that Drew thought she'd disgraced herself was a stinging, unwelcome slash at their recently built bridges. Suddenly she no longer felt hungry or willing to discuss anything calmly. She might never speak to him again. He assumed too quickly, and she wasn't one of his staff to command.

'I'm sorry, Libby.' He shook his head at himself as if it had just dawned on him that he'd been so darkly domineering. 'What I was trying to say is that the man is a danger, to himself and to others.

I'd hate him to involve you; you're too important for me to permit that.'

Libby sat slowly back down. She knew Zak was an idiot. But it was nice to be trusted and allowed to make up her mind.

'He caused a lot of carnage with his partying last night. Please forgive my bluntness, won't you?' Drew urged her to sit and she complied. But she felt her shaking fingers betray her as she put her sunglasses in their case.

Drew watched her intently. 'I shouldn't be taking this out on you. Zak Nazar is a drunk and a fool. My staff have been taking complaints and totting up damages all morning.'

'He was kind to me, and he's here alone too. There was nothing in it but being friendly.' Libby wanted to continue but held her rant when the waiter arrived to check on their meal. She kept her defence tight, not wanting to argue in front of Drew's staff. And the lawyer in her who still smarted wasn't ready to play along yet.

Seconds later, Drew removed his mobile phone and showed a picture on the screen that made her gasp. Carnage. Smashed glass. Tables overturned. Libby's eyes shot to meet his.

'Our ship's spa nearly shut today, as two beauticians are unable to work. There was damage to tables in the nightclub and glasses broken, plus a party that caused noise complaints. Performances in the bar. Zak treated our bar guests to a one-man entertainment extravaganza. And that's just the top line of his offences, in a single night.'

'I gave him a talking-to myself, but you've already decided I've sided with him.' She stared him out and added, 'I won't tolerate you telling me what to do. I've suffered that before from a man, and believe me, Zak is no more a partner in crime to me than I'm a trusted confidante to you. I think we should conclude this meal now.' She rose, her chair scraping on the floor.

Drew reached out. 'Maybe Zak

Nazar hasn't the monopoly share on idiocy after all. I was jealous that he managed to get your attention. I'm jealous when it comes to you.'

Anger dispersed with his open admission. Libby shook her head. 'Your captain's charm could do with a polish today.'

A heavy, loaded pause still hung between them. Drew's jaw was tight, but the creased skin around his eyes relaxed. 'We've had a number of crises on board. Two passengers passed away last night. Natural causes, but we also have an urgent engineering issue.' He held up a hand, palm out. 'We're still running. We also have an emerging fraud problem. So having some pompous-ass actor juggling champagne bottles was the last straw. I'm sorry I've put this all on you.'

Libby pushed against her temples. 'He juggled bottles?'

'Could have been a big hospital bill if it had gone wrong. The passenger-safety buck stops with me. You didn't deserve the blame. I'm the ass, not him.' He told her, 'I'm due back on the bridge shortly, and I've just ruined the most important appointment of my day. I'm so sorry.' He watched her, and his hesitant smile appeared. 'Our captain's dinner has been arranged for Thursday — if you'll still agree to come?'

She added, 'If you play nicely.'

'May I seek you out tonight? Usual place up on deck? I might even bring a picnic, so bypass the dessert trolley. That's not an order, just a suggestion.'

'You know where I sit to read. I'll leave the picnic up to you.' Maybe he'd been a bit of an idiot, but she'd had a window into the many and varied pressing challenges on a ship's captain's time. 'Second chance. Mess up at your peril.'

'I'm sorry, Libby. You mean more to me than all of it. Tonight I'll bring a picnic peace offering.'

Her heart jumped in a loop the loop of elation. The connection remained. And it fired off hopes inside her. David would never have backed down. Getting a confession that Drew was jealous and was sorry for his behaviour was something.

'I guess I'll have to pull all the stops out and show you I can do better,' he confided.

She'd give him another chance. Because she liked Drew's promise, and dearly wanted to dare to push for more.

6

The sun beat down on a new day in Cartagena, Spain. Libby enjoyed the sights before her in the port. Nearby market stalls beckoned and the buildings glowed brightly in stark, inviting welcome. No way would she let her turnaround with Drew drag on her vacation.

She set out with strong strides and looked forward to a day where she'd take her own instinctive steps, selecting somewhere for lunch herself. Her only tie was to be back at the boat by four, two hours before departure. She vowed to be there at least half an hour before curfew.

Libby wandered the cobbled alleys currently filled with other passengers. A few street changes soon found her surrounded with fewer tourists. Small craft stores and gastro food shops were a delight for her senses. She revelled in the sights and smells, indulging in souvenir knick-knacks.

She had almost convinced herself she'd take the 'scholarly' route of a cathedral visit next when a tiny shoe boutique ensnared her with its display. The to-die-for nude patent leather shoes centre stage beckoned, mainly due to the clear plastic heels scattered with stardust. Perfect for her cruise-ready peach evening dress for formal night. Expensive, but so worth it. She tossed the idea of the purchase over, then reminded herself David would have told her a firm no, and she vowed to try them on.

'Imagine bumping into you here,' a light voice said nearby. When Libby turned, Sienna stood grinning. 'Shoe shopping already?'

'Hi. Lovely to see you again.'

'You've found our secret hideaway. My husband must never know it's my Cartagena weakness. I have to hide the boxes.'

Libby shook her head dramatically. 'Not a peep from me.'

'And to make sure, we'll have to initiate you into their sublime secrets. Join us inside?' Another woman stood at Sienna's side. 'This is Maria, fellow ship's dancer and my shoe-shopping ally.' Sienna gushed over some shoes in the window. 'You must have an instinctive radar, and a good eye for shoes.'

So much for striking out on her own steam, but it felt so good to have company to shop with. 'Call it an untapped talent.' Libby bit her lip. 'I'm on holiday, and splurging is totally allowed.' Her glance returned to her dream shoes as she swallowed, knowing it was a decadent purchase. They really were drool-worthy. 'I'll bet they'd give me bunions.'

'Sacrilege! Don't dare back out or be a killjoy. You have to have them,' Sienna lambasted her. 'If you don't, you'll forever after regret it. That's how the law of sexy shoes works. Can you risk having that on your big-regrets bucket-list?'

'Sienna, you have serious shoe issues.'

'I know. My closet attests to it.'

'I think Hale probably knows without further evidence,' Libby whispered.

'So what are we waiting for?' Maria waggled her eyebrows in encourage-ment. 'Feels like destiny. And we're here to give the support you need.'

Sienna led the way, holding open the door. 'I don't care how much they cost. Shoes are the best souvenirs.'

'I'll probably only wear them once. Are you on commission?' Libby laughed. 'But I don't want to be trudging around with a shoebox all day.'

Sienna told her, 'Maria can twist men around her finger like greased castanets and speaks fluent Spanish. Watch and learn, my friend. She'll make sure transfer to the ship is included.'

Fifteen minutes later there were four pairs of shoes purchased and arrange-ments made for the store to return them to the ship. Maria, too, had splurged on some red sparkly stilettos, while Sienna had gone for soft suede ankle-caressing sandals. They were dancers; why wouldn't they?

Libby got her Cinderella shoes and an amazing pair of rose-gold shiny pumps. 'How did you manage to get him to oblige?' she asked.

They showed her with a wedge of leaflets in their bags. 'Said we'd tout the shop to passengers,' Sienna said. 'Leaflets on tables during our shows; the ladies will flock.'

'Ah! See you guys later,' said Libby. 'Thanks for your help.'

Sienna put a hand on her arm. 'Join us. Cartagena has the most Q-rated beaches in Spain. We planned a beach day and lunch. It's our day off, and Hale has to work, so this is girl time. Fancy joining in?'

No-brainer, thought Libby, finding herself smiling readily. 'If I can get swimwear. Didn't bring any.'

'More shopping.' Sienna screwed up

her nose. 'Come on, girlfriend. Let's get to it!'

★ ★ ★

A red and white natty swimsuit and nautical motif towel purchased, and Libby was set, though she had to put her foot down about a stunning '50s-style waist-clinching dress in a boutique. Admittedly it was gorgeous. They'd coerced her to try it on, and its pale pastel-pink colour had been tempting, but getting hampered by bags would be a mistake. She left the dress behind, justifying she had days for other boutiques in other ports. Though there was a twinge of remorse when she realised she'd have plenty of occasions to wear it on board.

As they walked back through the central square, amazing rhythms from a street performance of drummers and actors filled the air, enticing them closer. When they arrived in the square they saw that the troupe included stilt-walkers and people dressed in a flamboyant warrior style with bandanas and macho warrior dress. She had no idea what the spectacle commemorated, but it certainly had spirit.

The modern beat-centred music was highly infectious and the friends plunged into the crowd for a closer look, her dancer friends moving to the beat instinctively. Which turned out to be a potential bad move. Somehow in the space of a very short time, one of the burliest warrior performers, wearing a breastplate and fake skins, pulled Maria into their performance. At first she feigned declining, but before too long she played right along and eventually danced herself to great approval from the performers, who hadn't expected such a show. Maria was something in action. Libby clapped along, agog at how she moved, and she knew in this she wasn't alone.

And then a tiny feeling bugged her enough to look over each shoulder. If she wasn't mistaken, it felt as if she was being watched. But nobody stood out as she scanned the crowd. It was a weird feeling that stayed with her and made the hairs on her arms rise, but she dismissed it. She was probably just tired and in need of a café break.

A voice said beside her, 'You always end up in the thick of things, don't you?' Zak Nazar stood beside her, clapping and watching Maria with raw appreciation.

A part of Libby relaxed inside with relief that it must have been Zak who gave her the observed feeling. 'I could say the same for you,' she teased.

'I like to think I'm a man who gets to where the action is.'

'Don't we know it,' Libby replied, then noted he wasn't listening to her. His attention was elsewhere, riveted to a woman with great moves as well as superlative taste in shoes.

'Who is that wondrous creature?' he whispered.

'Maria. Ship's dancer. Caught your eye?'

'I'd be made of stone not to notice. A very fine señorita indeed,' he whispered. 'But she'd never look at a rogue like me.'

'You're a celebrity, and ship's rebel bad boy. You think you deserve such a prize?'

His face showed hurt, and Libby regretted her teasing words. 'The other night she gave me the cold shoulder. It's why I got drunk.'

'Ah.' Libby sighed, then added, 'I'm going to the beach with her later. Want me to put a word in?'

Zak meekly smiled. 'I seem to have a habit of late of turning the nice girls off. Take plenty of photographs. I can dream.' He slipped into the crowd after waving goodbye. He may ham up the rogue vibe, but he was a great guy really, she thought.

Libby clapped as Maria finished her impromptu flamenco, surrounded by applauding stilt-walkers and an enthralled audience. She snapped photos for Zak, collecting great pictures of the girls and their clan of Spanish Viking brigands. Libby nudged Sienna to take centre stage and Sienna didn't need asking twice. She twisted and danced and went into a routine that drew gasps and appreciative clapping from all around.

Libby took more album photos. This was what vacations were about — the kind of freeing experience she'd craved; yet David would have hated it. He'd have pulled her away, telling her how unseemly the rabble were, not caring if she itched to enjoy the scene.

At the end of the dance, Libby was approached by the biggest Spanish Viking, wearing a horned hat, flamboyant moustache and muscles fit for TV wrestling.

'Señorita? *Vamos!*' He spoke fast Spanish Libby didn't understand, and took her hand, then picked her up and carried her around like flotsam, handing her camera to someone else. While her instincts yearned to retreat from the crazy scene, she laughed along.

'Never a dull moment with you two,' she shouted down to her friends.

But shouldn't she be grateful? She could right now be on a tour of the cathedral in hushed voices, as David would have decreed; but instead she was part of the action, experiencing joyful times with amazing friends. The crazy theatrical street rabble dispersed, leaving her on an endorphin high. 'That was incredible! Crazy, but such fun!'

'We thought it was you!' said a loud, unmistakable voice. Edna Randall stood with hands on hips. 'We're having a drink with our friends The Fosters from Surrey, England. Come and join us!'

'Hey, Libby, sweetheart. Come join us?' As soon as Libby saw Walt, wearing a Spanish flag baseball cap and waving at her in joy, her heart softened and she pulled Maria and Sienna along.

They opted for iced lemon water and were soon chatting. Valerie and Harry Foster looked dressed ready for posh VIP golf. They'd mastered his-and-hers preppy plaid-plus knitwear done by the book: same sweaters in complementary colours, and matching trousers. The statement opal necklace Valerie wore with her lilac golf gear was, however, as bling as the sport ever got. Their sunglasses were his-and-hers sports shades, but their warm and friendly manner made Libby thoroughly glad the Randalls had found friends more in keeping with their years. It would keep Edna out of her business.

'You enjoying your time on board *Oceana Onyx*?' Libby asked.

The woman's eyes widened. 'I am indeed,' said Valerie in rapture. 'The food is sublime. But my favourite thing of all is formal night. My only problem will be choosing which evening gown. And my jewels! I've brought so many.' She touched her neck, and the enormous flower-shaped gem ring sparkled its presence. Valerie took great pride in being a carnival of cabochon.

'I only brought one dress,' Libby admitted.

'You'll have to remedy that, dear,'

Edna advised. 'If I had a figure like yours, I'd flaunt it left, right and centre.'

'Be grateful she hasn't,' Walt added softly. 'She'd be wearing flamenco frocks day and night!'

'Your necklace is stunning,' Libby remarked to Valerie. 'It's the loveliest thing I've ever seen. I can't wait to see your other pieces.'

'Thank you. You must dress up, Libby. It's what cruising is about, and I'm a huge cruise fan. This is my fifteenth and counting.'

Her comment recalled the dress Libby had drooled over. Maybe she should have bought it; then she could wear that when she dined with Drew, and save her peach chiffon number for formal night. Decisions, decisions. And crazy thoughts, given that she and Drew were more off than on.

'We love to dine at the captain's table,' Valerie continued. 'Captain Muldoon has to be the most attractive captain I've ever had the pleasure to meet, and believe me I'm a cruise veteran. But enough of me — today is Walt and Edna's day. It's their anniversary. We've booked a table in a nearby hotel for a special lunch. On us, of course. Imagine, fifty years of wedded bliss!'

'Edna and Walt, why didn't you say?' challenged Libby. She felt remiss that she'd been unaware. The Randalls had kept this quiet. And she was surprised they hadn't told her.

'We don't need fuss!' Edna claimed. Though knowing Edna, Libby wondered why she'd opted for low-key.

'Aren't you having a special dinner on board?'

'No, dear. Walt doesn't like fuss. He just wants our celebration to be quiet.'

Which bemused Libby more. She couldn't imagine Walt saying no to his wife on such an important occasion. So why the changed approach? She knew they were in the cheaper budget cabin. She'd also observed that they were always on the lookout for best-value freebies on board. Libby felt saddened and vowed to discover if she could help somehow.

She drained her glass and winked at her friends. 'We mustn't delay these special celebrations. And we need to claim our spot on the beach. Ready to go get a cab now?'

Again she turned, convinced that someone was nearby and watching. She'd never in her life felt that way before. It was as inexplicable as it was unsettling. Yet all around her no one took any notice, and she felt foolish for her mistake.

'Ready to hit the sand and surf and drink in those rays,' Sienna said. Laughing, they went off together, leaving the Randalls and Fosters waving after them.

★ ★ ★

Libby forked her salad while relaxing in the beachside café. The dressing was delicious, but pacing herself was vital.

She'd dinner to get through, and she'd also made secret picnic plans with Drew.

'A little bird told me they saw you brunching with our esteemed captain today. Did the lovely Libby enjoy herself?' Sienna asked, winking and grinning.

'Just a friendly brunch. No biggie. Two people eating. It is allowed.'

'We don't believe you. News circulates faster aboard our ship than wasps around an ice-cream cart. We know the big man on deck gave you special attention.'

Libby felt her face heat. It wasn't the sun. And as much as she wanted girl talk about her Drew views, could she venture there? He was, after all, their boss. Should she be talking private life with them?

But Sienna beat her to it. 'Come on, Libby. You can trust us. We know he has the hots for you, and don't worry. Maria's dating our chief chef Julio. What's gossiped in private stays in private. We have strict codes.'

'Zak will be gutted. He has the hots for Maria,' Libby let his confession slip.

'Not my type. And no competition when Julio makes desserts like a chocolate magician!' Maria gushed, and they all laughed.

'You two are a force in itself. And poor Zak is in for disappointing news,' Libby added.

'So,' Maria probed, 'do you like him? We've never seen him this way with anyone.'

'I hardly know what to think.' But she threw caution to the wind and went on to explain their brunch date gone wrong, and her gripes at his assumptions that she needed moral direction when it came to Zak. She also explained about how she did like Drew; that they went way back and had history.

'We dated. After only six months he popped the question, and I was beyond happy. But I was always getting into muddles; I was too in awe of him. I thought it was too soon to propose. If I'm honest, I thought he was way out of my league — good-looking, charming, fit, and a sweetheart too. I could see women admiring him and felt like a nerdy solicitor workaholic. And the harder I tried to shake my doubts, the more I made a fool of myself. We split, but there were issues because I did it badly.'

Sienna reassured her, 'Hale and I are chalk and cheese, but it works. There's no such thing as a perfect relationship.'

'It does matter when you're working round the clock to get your first law job off the ground. I got an amazing chance with a big firm. And I sidelined Drew in favour of my career to the point that I gave his mother food poisoning. At the end of the day, our small issues added up, so we broke up.'

'But you're so confident, so sensible. So successful. What's to doubt now?' Maria said.

'My job takes a lot of hours. I don't have much free time, or confidence outside of work. And I'm not the type of person who graces a man's arm. That's what Drew needed, I sensed. A glam girl with charm and ease.'

The women looked at each other and shared a glance Libby didn't understand. 'Maybe you have Drew more wrong than you know,' Sienna said. 'His prior relationship left him heartbroken.'

'Ah, Josie. Well the cancer situation would be arduous. Who could blame him?'

'There's way more to it than that, Libby. But it's Drew who should tell you about that. Just don't go imagining Josie was saintly. She was loud. Wacky. And she was very much in charge. Sure she was glam, but she was very strong-minded too. Drew was left reeling, but not in the ways you may think.'

More confused than ever, Libby deduced she should try to change the topic. 'What about you, Sienna? Tell me all about your wedding.'

'The wedding was all I dreamed it

should be. And now I just want to quit cruising and give it up to have lots of his babies and be happy!'

Maria nodded and shrugged in a 'tell me something I don't know' move.

Libby answered, 'I thought you'd be committed to cruising for years ahead.'

'We're already trying for baby number one. I'm crossing fingers and toes and so is he. Can't wait. Libby, think back to that making-an-assumption thing. You thought something about me that wasn't the case. Maybe you need to think about that with other things, like you and Drew being incompatible?'

'Drew is still out of my league, though. That hasn't changed.'

Sienna said to Maria, 'She needs us to work on her. But I'm pretty sure with a bit more investment in shoes, dresses and make-up we'll have it cracked. When are you seeing each other again?' she asked Libby.

'A picnic,' said Libby, feeling the blushes consume her.

'You should have bought that dress.'

'Not for a picnic.'

'No, silly. For the other opportunities to knock his socks off. You make a habit of leaving things behind that you should have had the courage to go for.'

Libby ignored her obvious Drew push, and pushed on herself. 'I sense a campaign.'

'He's my husband's bestie. If we go now, we can wait in the cab while you buy it. The dress is calling — I hear it from here . . . '

Libby already knew she'd have to go back to Cartagena and seek it out before she went back to the ship.

'See?' said Maria. 'You should have listened to your fairy godmothers. That's a learning curve you need to consider.'

'Slow learner,' said Libby, bagging her towel and beach stuff on fast speed. 'I should have, but stop badgering me and let's go and say yes to the dress.'

* * *

Drew and his management team left the meeting room, and Drew took his security specialist to his office near the bridge. The recent intelligence made grim listening. They had a problem on board. Theft. Card fraud. System hacks. Suspicions cabin thefts too. And some incidents in ports that suggested leaked intelligence. All underway on this very trip on board his ship. The knowledge left Drew feeling both devastated that this should happen on his watch, and determined to get to the nub of the criminality as soon as possible.

Zander Hughes walked beside him. He had faith in this new addition to the team — albeit sent by HQ. 'We've made a good start on interception of the perpetrators. Be reassured that we're quite a few steps ahead of them on this. We'll catch them, trust in it. They won't realise we know yet.'

'I feel under mutiny,' Drew answered, his jaw clenching; and though he scanned the ocean, he didn't see the usual majestic swell. Today he merely felt betrayed by dark danger that lurked beneath the surface. Just as was the case on this ship.

'Same thing has been happening on several of the cruise liners in the fleet. Cybercrime is commonplace these days. Stands to reason that a liner this size will always have a criminal element. It's unfortunate that it's all hitting at once for you.'

Drew shook his head vehemently. 'Not among my staff. Not until now.'

'We can't be sure it's all a staff issue. Could be one or two rogue employees and some coincidental additional crime. Don't make more of this than needs be. We're on top of it. Trust in our ability to conquer.'

'It's still unsettling. This is a career first and not a good one.'

Zander assured him, 'Stay vigilant. We'll have a communications crackdown to notify staff to be vigilant of passengers. We won't alert them to the staff-problem suspicions. But it'll keep the team on board. And some new systems will be put in place for fraud detection. Heightened CCTV. Trust that by this week, the noose will be tight and we'll be making headway.'

Drew could only hope Zander was proven right, because a swift resolution was paramount. But at this point, it felt too distant and beyond his control.

* * *

Something causing crowds of people had cut off the central streets, and Cartagena traffic was gridlocked. It proved to be a demonstration. Normally Libby would have cried off and dismissed the dress as a bad idea had she known this, but once they were surrounded by stuck traffic it was too late to rethink. She'd forever think of it as the dress of doom.

'I'm sorry, ladies. I hadn't realised this might all go wrong.'

'You weren't to know,' Sienna reassured her. 'Fortunately my hubby won't let him leave port without us. At least, I hope he won't.' She bit her lip in a tell-tale gesture. 'It's never happened before; we haven't dared to be late. I think I'll be in trouble, though.'

Libby gasped, 'I'd hate to be responsible.'

'I'll call ahead,' said Sienna, getting out her phone and dialling. 'I'll explain to Hale and he'll clear things. There are plusses to being married to the second officer.'

'Why don't we get out and run back? There's time,' said Libby.

'We haven't wasted this time sitting here to go home empty-handed. Get the dress.'

'You have to be kidding me,' said Libby.

Sienna opened the door and got out to allow her to follow suit. 'Go. Run as fast as you can, get it and then run back to port.'

Sienna paid the cab driver and told Libby to head for the boutique, giving directions too speedily for her to properly absorb. She'd itched to run back to ship with them and should have gone with instinct, because pretty soon the route she remembered from the morning wasn't easy to recognise. She couldn't get her bearings no matter how she tried, and when she asked people in the street they didn't speak enough English.

After nearly giving up, somehow Libby recognised a shop close by and then the street with the dress shop. She bought the dress in record time and was about to start feeling better when she looked at her watch. It was already ten to four. Passengers were always told latest time to embark was two hours before the ship left dock. She'd be in trouble. All for the sake of a fashion mistake.

Libby sped harum-scarum down the street, aiming to run as fast as she could to get back. She'd be a sweaty wreck but it would be worth it. And then it happened in a blur. She was running one moment, and then the next she was flat on her behind on the cobblestones, her bags on the ground beside her and a bruise on her arm from where someone had charged fully into her, knocking her to the ground. They'd tried to snatch her bag but she'd held on with grim determination, and they must have given up and taken off, because all she saw was a dark jacket and trousers disappearing.

By the time she rose and tried to look properly, her assailant was a speck in the distance. Libby rubbed her sore flesh and struggled to rise. The strap on her bag was now broken, and she'd definitely be late. And if she wasn't mistaken, her ankle throbbed. So much for investing in teetering stilettos. Her folly was all too patent.

Just then a car stopped beside her, beeping its horn. Sitting in disarray, she saw the window wind down. Lolling on the back seat was, of all people, Zak. 'What happened?' he asked. 'You okay?'

Libby struggled to know exactly. 'I only saw him for a second. He tried to snatch my bag. My ankle is swelling up like a balloon.'

Zak got out of his cab and helped with her bags. 'You sure you're okay?'

'I think so. Sore ankle and a few bruises.'

'Let's get you inside. I owe you a favour. And the girls told me they'd left you out alone. Now I'm glad I did come to find you.'

Libby gingerly clambered into the cab, gratified that although she was late, it could have been much worse. 'You saved my neck.'

'Ditto, Libby. I'm so sorry for what I put you though. I've been such an ass. I apologise for being a loose cannon and not taking your comments about my conduct in good spirit. I've already laid it on thick with the captain and his team. You were right — I acted like an idiot.'

'Apology accepted,' she said, glad that in less than a minute she'd be back aboard the ship. Leaving the cab, they both slowly made their way back, Zak taking care of her bags, and the sight ahead of her made Libby's mouth dry and her stomach freefall.

Drew stood with his arms crossed beside his ship, face tensed, expression stern. She'd have chanced a smile at him but she doubted it would make impact. She was somewhat upturned from the pavement fall, and ever since tears had inched closer to the surface.

'Sorry, I got held up in traffic and had to run. Zak picked me up.'

Zak interjected, 'What she's omitted to say is that some thief threw her on the pavement and tried to snatch her bag.'

'Are you okay?' Drew's brow creased and his gaze searched hers.

'My ankle's tender.'

'Let's get you to the medical room,' he said simply. But the look he cast was grim. Libby guessed he'd be displeased that Zak was with her. Drew probably thought they'd been drinking in a tapas bar together.

'Thank you for rescuing her,' he

quietly told Zak, then turned back to Libby. 'You could have been robbed. Or worse. Please keep with a friend during shore excursions. I'm only sorry that I didn't entrust you to Zak's care sooner.'

Not just an epic climb-down — a huge surprise.

Drew explained, 'An onlooker saw the incident and called her husband, who's a policeman. Thanks to Zak helping you, she had time to take action. They hope to apprehend your assailant.' His expression turned into a brief flash of smile.

Libby turned to her champion 'Thanks, Zak. Your help was much appreciated. And Drew, I'm sorry to have delayed your ship.'

'You're important guests. Of course you realise I'll have to insist on strict future rules for your safety.'

Libby felt like her life had turned into a fast-paced comic-strip novel with too many twists. David would have been appalled. She couldn't keep up either.

As Drew pulled her into the warm

comforting cave of his broad chest, Zak took a step back. 'I'll give you two good people privacy,' he said, coughing lightly on his fist.

'Thanks, Zak. Appreciated.' Then Drew turned to her. 'You didn't think I'd leave without you?'

'Zak's not so very bad at heart,' Libby whispered.

'He's already proved his contrition to me. I give second chances when I think they're deserved. And when I'm wrong, I say it. I misjudged him.'

'You're pretty great too, my captain crusader,' Libby answered. He proved her right when he tenderly kissed her. His lips were warm and smooth and he smelled heavenly. Though the kiss was chaste, it left her buzzing, most especially from the contact of his hand on the small of her back. This one small kiss held startling promise.

Her gaze rose to his when he said, 'I like rescuing you. Though I think Zak was the real hero today.'

'I'll be the judge of that, Captain,' she

7

Drew palmed the back of his neck, thanking heaven that at least he had Libby to keep him grounded. The only thing making his day bearable had been brunch with her, but he'd screwed it up monumentally — which he really hoped he might have rallied back from with his impromptu kiss. She'd certainly responded positively. He also hoped the surprise he had in store would make it up to her. And he wondered how she'd become his emotional life raft all of a sudden.

The sight of her caused his breath to catch. Curled up on her usual steamer chair, she made his inner GPS go crazy finding her for precious time alone. He took several seconds to drink in the view. Blanket firmly in place, his e-reader on her lap, Libby beckoned him like a moth to a lamp. She radiated welcome light and a pinch of indefinable Libby magic.

Drew knew he could have sought out his chef and made a showy spread to impress, but he'd opted for a low-key private picnic. He grinned. Reaching her, he offered his wicker basket and was rewarded with her spellbinding smile.

'So what's in there?' she asked, and laid her things aside then crossed her hands.

'Surprise,' he teased. 'How's the ankle?'

She showed her foot. 'Swelling's improved; ice pack took the edge off. Arnica and ibuprofen helped. And by the way, I met Lilly Lazlo. I think Lilly's just going along with her dad's wishes, actually, if we get to the nub of things.'

Drew sat down beside her. 'More of that later. May I begin?' He laid down his hamper.

She beckoned him to sit. 'I ate sensibly so I'd have room. This had better be good to have warranted me shunning the sweet trolley. There were profiteroles tonight.'

'I'll try not to disappoint.' Drew sat, enjoying the lightness of her mood.

'Stop keeping me waiting.'

'All in good time.' He produced the ceramic burner and lit a candle, then presented a pot of melted pure chocolate. The platter of fruit, brownie and blondie chunks and marshmallows got a low whistle. 'Did I impress?'

'How could I not be?'

Drew tried not to drool when she navigated a chocolate-dipped marsh-mallow between her lips. A tremor of desire twisted at the sight. He speared a strawberry and tried to do the same, just as Libby sent a trail of hot chocolate over the back of his arm. Thankfully he wore short-sleeved shirts.

She gasped.

'It's fine,' he assured her. But the heat came from her impact. He saw Libby watch him wipe the chocolate from his arm with a silk handkerchief.

'That's a disgraceful waste of chocolate. Think of the laundry room too.'

They ate in silence, enjoying the tastes.

'You should never waste something so good,' she said.

He knew she was right. They'd had something good but had wasted their chance. If only they'd tried to salvage what they'd had.

'You passed the picnic test with honours.' The sparks in her eyes told him she meant it: he'd finally hit on a winning recipe with Libby.

'Lilly's not as keen on law as Dad thinks?' he asked.

She shook her head. 'She's crazy about police work.'

'Seriously? Her dad is in law enforcement himself.'

'Absolutely. Her dad's been a detective for a long time and he's against the choice. I have a hunch that's the crux of the problem.'

'Do you think it would help if I talk to him?' Drew offered.

'Let me talk to her some more. I promised we'd meet again. I have a few ideas about coaching her to come clean. I also need to ask a favour, Drew,' she ventured. 'The Randalls celebrated a special anniversary but in a low-key way today. Who should I speak with to make arrangements for a surprise?'

Drew watched her. 'Let me know what you'd like done and I'll make it happen.'

'I'd be happy to pay for them to have a special meal. They're a nice couple. Edna is overbearing but she means well, and Walt is a sweetheart. Fifty years of marriage all told.' Libby explained her wish for them to have champagne and flowers delivered too.

'So how about I invite them to a special captain's dinner? Would that be appropriate?'

The suggestion of Drew's was perfect. 'Edna would be over the moon.'

Drew agreed to take care of arrangements. Sitting there as if the ship's captain had illicit picnics in dark solitude every day of the week, he was struck by the thought that this was probably rare behaviour for him.

She added, 'Edna's completely in awe of you.'

He scoffed. 'Would tomorrow night be working too fast for your plans?'

'Amazing. But keep it a surprise. Maybe a personal invitation from you?'

Drew paused. 'You'll join us too?'

'Of course. If that's okay with you.' She watched him press his lips together as if to seal the plan.

'More than okay. Is there no end to my efforts to impress you ... ? You always did know how to keep me grounded, Lib. You shunned the VIP stuff. It's one of the reasons I liked you so much. It contrasted with my family.'

'Your mother and brother, you mean.'

Drew's mother had made no secret of her lofty aims for her family; it was one of the reasons Libby had been so keen to impress her. Though Libby imagined she must be pretty impressed by Drew's career heights now. His other brother had been something of a musical protégé.

'My mother's always liked my brother the best. You never did get the chance to meet Hal. He always had concert obligations with his touring.'

'He was a busy concert pianist musician. He still in the big time?'

Drew nodded. 'Bigger than ever. With my mother as controlling manager, how could he not be? They love the finer things. Me, I was never bothered, so it's crazy that I'm cruising in five-star luxury now. That was never my scene.'

Libby faked a stern expression. 'You're the one who's five-star. Your heart's high-class.'

His grin drifted into a thoughtful stare. Libby felt grateful for his help. And now she had the full window on his self-deprecating style. His background — mum and brother with eyes firmly on the prize of fame — had moulded him. Maybe made him rebel, or retreat. She itched to explore further but sensed now wasn't the time.

Libby confided, 'I really appreciate your help more than you know.'

'On that note, I need to apologise,' he replied. 'As I said earlier, I was wrong about Zak. I assumed he'd be a demanding high-maintenance star. But he's down to earth when you dig deeper. I'm grateful he looks out for you.'

She contemplated his comments. 'Maybe I shouldn't have got so uppity before; Zak abused his position.'

'Wrecking our brunch date was never the right course of action.' Drew's eyes sparkled, then his expression grew serious. 'As with Hal, I was put out and jealous. In my defence, I was also stressed with work. But I did you a disservice. I came on strong. Please forgive me.'

A feeling of contentment and gratitude swirled inside of Libby. She knew he meant it deeply, and respected him all the more for the confidences. 'I spent too long in a previous relationship staying silent in my disquiet. The new Libby speaks out. I'd already left Zak in no doubt of my views. You assuming I was cosying up to his stardom was off-beam. I'm my own woman, Drew, and I tell it like it is.' *Except when it comes to my captain crush.*

Drew watched her, his expression serious. 'Zak tells me he's come here to get over a broken heart. He's lost his home, and his girlfriend made it brutally public.'

'You and Zak talked? So you've bonded?'

'Men do talk, you know.' Drew shrugged his shoulders. 'I invited him to use his VIP gym pass when I do, to help for his next movie role. He has a big action role lined up. He's channelling his feelings positively with a gym kick.' Drew grinned.

'A shrewd move.'

'I like to think I'm pretty switched on. I invited you out and apologised, didn't I?'

Libby nodded. 'And you don't have to live up to your mother and brother's high-brow tastes. You're pretty great as you are.'

'I like 'new Libby' too.' He took her hand. 'Does telling things like they are include telling me about our chances of an 'us'?'

Thrills multiplied, making her feel almost giddy and excited to see where the moment led. Drew moved closer, capturing her gaze with his. She liked inhaling his inviting scent; enjoyed the way their legs touched. With a soft touch he stroked her face.

'The sweetest part of this date is you,' Drew whispered. And with a gentle movement of his head closing the space and his lips slanting to cover hers, he kissed her. 'Don't say I'm off course.'

'As usual, you're in full impeccable control.'

So he kissed her again. And this time the caress reversed the years. Drew Muldoon had always been a sensational kisser. The zinging sparks inside her told her he'd improved. Why had she ever walked away from this?

'I'm still interested. I've wanted to do that since we met again,' Drew admitted, and stared into her eyes with intensity. 'I'm glad you're here. And I'm especially glad you no longer avoid me.'

'You're more fun under moonlight.' She pulled him back to take a kiss of her own and prove he wasn't the only one enjoying the moment to the max.

The brisk, urgent tone of Drew's phone pulled Libby out of his embrace with as much reluctance as surprise.

'Great timing,' he muttered. 'Muldoon. Where? I'm on it. Be right there.' The dreamy bubble of their on-deck tryst popped with the urgency in his response. Already on his feet, Drew said, 'I have to go. Sorry, no time to explain.'

'No problem,' Libby answered. Deflation swept through her. Then she was ultra-surprised when he turned back and pulled her into his strong, warm arms again. He kissed her so tenderly it caused a melt response and a deep sense of joy to unfurl inside her. 'To keep me going until the end of the shift. See you tomorrow. We have a dinner date, remember?'

So it was with surprise when only ten minutes later the female officer she'd bumped into the first day she'd ventured onto the officer's deck appeared. 'Ms. Grant? The captain asks you to accompany me. There's an incident involving your friends. Don't panic. We think you'll be a good person to provide support.'

'Walt and Edna?' Libby tensed. 'What's happened?'

'Captain Muldoon's asked for you to help calm Mrs Randall. Their friends the Fosters have been involved in an incident. She's somewhat overwrought. He knows she'll listen to you.'

Libby rose and was already walking, leaving her belongings behind. She'd fetch them later. 'I don't like the sound of that.'

Valerie Foster sat ashen-faced and stiff-backed in a chair with a brandy in hand. She looked like she'd seen two ghosts at once while Edna Randall wailed noisily nearby.

'What's happened?' asked Libby. 'Oh dear. The cabin's in disarray.' The room was so trashed it was a superfluous comment. Drawers had been pulled free of their cabinets and emptied. Pillows lay tossed on the floor.

Edna's imperious tone told Libby she was currently on the taut zip-wire of her frayed nerves. 'All her precious jewels are gone! On-board theft! Personal irreplaceable items all taken. How are we supposed to sleep safely in our beds?'

Walt was nowhere to be seen, and he was usually the one who fine-tuned his wife's reactions. With Drew and another man Libby took as a security guard outside the cabin door, along with the Fosters and Edna plus herself, the strident emotions filled the small space and made thought impossible.

Libby moved to lower the stress level. 'Edna, why don't I take you to your cabin?'

'How can I sleep with all this? I don't feel safe. We should vacate at the next port. Can't a helicopter airlift us to safety?'

Drew flashed Libby a look she read as 'intervention time' and she guided her elderly friend by the elbow. 'Let's get you a nice drink on deck while the officers investigate. Meanwhile, why don't you tell me the full details?' The female officer caught her eye and winked that she'd navigated well.

Edna objected, 'How am I to bear it?'

'Calm down, dear,' came Walt's voice from the corridor. 'Libby's an attorney and talks sense. She's used to dealing with crises, and she wants your version of events. You'll be helping enquiries.'

It was a line which Edna thankfully swallowed whole. Libby kept her hold on Edna, guiding her to calmer waters at Walt's side. She soothed softly, 'Their possessions will be insured. And as upsetting as that all is, things can be replaced. Nobody's hurt. Strikes me a ship is a good place to catch a thief.'

Unfortunately the words didn't calm Edna. She pushed her handkerchief to her mouth. 'How do you do that job of yours, dealing with common criminals?'

'Contract law is a very different world. But in theory it's all about right and wrong. We'll catch the scoundrel — count on it.' Libby saw Drew cast her a wry look. She wondered who had the harder job to face.

★ ★ ★

Hesitating before knocking on Libby's cabin door, Drew sucked in a breath. What a night. Inside the cabin he heard movement and felt his heart race.

'It's Drew. Sorry to disturb you.'

'You're fine.' She opened the door, and even the hint of a smile with tired eyes had his heart zooming all around his ribcage. That and the sight of her checked pyjamas.

'You've had a long day,' he remarked.

'This vacation thing is so taxing,' she jested. 'Actually, it's Edna I'm worried about. She's taken it badly. Hardly an ideal climax to special anniversary celebrations. Want to come in? It's small, but you could just about swing a cat if they were allowed on board.'

He walked in and closed the door softly, then took in her sweet floral scent that teased him. The little personal touches in the room had him hooked. Her peachy silk robe cast across the end of the bed. Her scent bottles and a writing journal laid nearby.

'May I sit? Do you mind? Order has been restored.'

'Of course you can. Good, I'm glad.'

He sat on the chair in the cabin corner and composed himself before charting a new conversation course. 'They were robbed during dinner. Room messed up and all valuables taken. Cameras, a phone. Wallets. Jewellery mainly — and she had a lot of it. We've sealed off the room; police will be involved, but my security official is already scanning CCTV. Irreparable damage done to the trust of two pairs of loyal repeat-booking guests. That's the sad part.'

'And how are the Fosters now?'

'Remarkably calm. Transferred to a VIP cabin. Fortunately we had a vacancy. They seem to be coping better than Edna, considering what they've lost. How was she?'

He watched Libby rub her temples. She looked tired. 'Two brandies mellowed her in the end. I don't think she was ready to have her faith in happy cruising shattered.'

Drew's frustration cycloned, and he hoped it wasn't too evident as he wanted Libby to feel he had it all under control. 'Please trust that the perpetrator will be held to account. Make no mistake, Libby, I intend to make sure the criminals pay. Thanks for stepping in. Hope you didn't mind me involving you? I know you've steered Edna right before.'

She smiled at him and his heart flipped over. 'I'm more than happy to help. I feel for them all.'

'I hope this won't ever be repeated. Actually, we have fresh leads. We have suspicions these aren't isolated incidents. We've had a spate of on-board fraud and crime and we think this could be tied in. Please keep that information confidential. Rest assured, we're closing the net.'

'Does this mean our dinner date is on hold?'

Drew shook his head. 'No. It's more pressing now. To mellow Edna. And as a gesture to the Fosters. Have faith, we're working hard to draw all this nasty business to a close. Ibiza tomorrow. I've asked Zak to chaperone you. Given current issues, I'd rather you were safe and had company. Do you mind me doing that without asking?'

'I don't plan more run-ins with

muggers. But that's kind. Thanks.'

The thought scared him more than she knew. 'I want all my passengers safe, but most especially you,' he said, drawing her close to kiss her forehead and briefly touch her hair. She smelled amazing. 'Your welfare is paramount. You matter to me. Enjoy Ibiza. I wish it was me taking you there instead of Zak.'

From the way he kissed her, he hoped she had no doubt he meant it, and that he'd work full speed ahead to solve the problems aboard his ship so that once again he could focus on the wonderful woman who'd walked back onto his horizon.

8

After a night of feeling well slept and blissed out by Drew's kisses, an unexpected knock sounded on Libby's cabin door next morning.

'Libby Grant?' The purser asked, passing her a note. As soon as she opened it, Libby saw that it came from her friend Chrissie Michaels back in London.

'Your friend asks you to call urgently; she's left several messages already.' The purser's smile suggested he'd got a good dose of assertive Chrissie already. 'She was insistent you call her today.'

'I'm sure she was, if I know Chrissie. Thanks. I'll call now. She's a lady who doesn't like to be kept waiting.'

But Libby also knew Chrissie was no drama queen. She figured that with a shore trip planned to Ibiza on today's schedule, she'd better handle it now.

The Lena Lounge was a quiet area where the ship boasted best mobile phone reception. It proved deserted, as only the early breakfast risers were about when she got there. The smells from the dining area were enticing.

Her friend answered in minimal rings. 'Hey, Lib. Great to hear your voice.'

'Chrissie. What's up?'

Chrissie gasped on a breathless rush. 'I've been bursting to talk. How's the vacation?'

'It's great. But forget that. Nothing bad happened, I hope?' Concern tugged inside her for answers.

Chrissie's pause lingered. 'The opposite. It's big news, as in getting married in a full-on down on one knee, ring hidden in a glass of champagne, serenading mariachi band proposal!' She squealed then elaborated. 'Freddie popped the question at a swanky London restaurant. The ring's the size of Jupiter; must've cost the earth, but he can afford it, given he's landed gentry! So just that kind of news. Bet you never planned on being a bridesmaid this year?'

'Chris, I'm so happy for you! And relieved. Wow, when will it be?'

'As soon as possible. I needed to tell you because I can't set the date unless I know you're free. We want to go for two months' time. Twentieth, as that's when the stately home is available for a do that big. We're talking the works — estate chapel and a huge banquet.'

'What can I say? Except whatever it takes, I'll be there. Wouldn't miss it.'

Chrissie went on, 'Can you believe, me dressed up like a duchess parading through an old pile of English stately home history? I can save the full story. Just wanted to you to be available. Say you'll help us?'

Libby hugged the news tight. 'He's the one getting a treasure. Of course I'm in. Just keep my secretary in the loop. And be kind with the dress choice; no Scarlett O'Hara.'

Chrissie's laughter rattled down the

line. 'I'll do better than that. Hope your cruise experience is all you dreamed it would be. Hope you're letting your hair down too.'

'It's the trip I'm here for, and it's incredible; so much still to see. I look forward to every new port of call. But I can save all that for my return.' Libby kept her Drew secret to herself. The last thing she needed was Chrissie demanding a full run-down. And their relationship was still fragile in her mind. Yet of all things, that felt like what she needed — to talk to a friend about right now. Just then, Lilly Lazlo appeared in the doorway, but hung back.

Libby confided softly in a whisper, 'I've got to go. Let's just say the captain has caught my eye. I'll save the rest for another time.'

'You're a terrible tease! Bring him to the wedding as your plus-one.'

Libby replaced the receiver, hiding her grin from Chrissie's last comment, and Lilly soon approached her.

'I need to talk.'

'Take a seat, Lilly. If it's about your concerns regarding your course . . . '

Lilly's expression was grave and her eyes were wide. 'It's nothing to do with that. The couple that had their room robbed last night — I think I might have seen who did it. I've tossed and turned about it, but now I think I'm sure.'

Libby couldn't quite believe what she was hearing, but didn't doubt Lilly's sincerity. The girl was obviously shaken and worried, and she was twisting the friendship bracelet around her wrist so tightly Libby thought it would break and scatter beads if she kept it up.

'You saw someone go in?' Libby asked softly.

'No. I tried to. But I heard a conversation.'

'Tell me more.'

'There's a woman on board my dad knows. They've met several times and I've kept watch in secret. At first I was worried he's found a new woman. My mum passed away five years ago; I'd imagined he's still grieving. Then this trip made me think otherwise. He slips out late at night, or tells me he's going for a walk and disappears.'

'And you followed?'

'A few times. I saw them together. I've been sneaking around to try and find out more. Please don't tell my dad. I did it for good reasons.'

Libby shook her head. 'Of course I won't. Anything you tell me stays confidential. But what does this have to do with the robbery? And how did you know about it?'

'We're in the cabin near the security office. We couldn't help but notice the goings on last night. I slipped out of the room after Dad left to see what was up. I saw officers crowded around a cabin on the deck below. Then I hid out in the corner of the reading lounge. Sometimes Dad meets the woman there.'

Libby took a breath. 'Listen, Lilly. Life isn't a game or a TV crime drama. You could get in serious trouble hiding and eavesdropping on conversations on your own like that.'

'Dad didn't appear. But another guy did, and he was calling someone. He said he had things under control and that the person on the line should meet him in twenty minutes. He said he'd had the key card delivered, and I distinctly heard him say the Fosters were at dinner. Then he said, 'Do they have the rubies yet? Why not? Are they stupid?' Then he hung up and left, so I followed.'

'Lilly, I don't like the sound of this. And it worries me that you did that.'

'Surely he must be on CCTV, because I saw him go there before I hid.'

'Did you see him come back out?'

'I didn't hang around. I went straight back to find my dad. If he'd met up with his lady friend, he didn't say. I couldn't work it into the conversation. I'm getting so confused and frustrated with the whole situation.'

'Lilly, promise me — no more acting

on hunches?' The look on Lilly's face made Libby worry she'd been too censuring. 'It's great that you've told me all this. Would you mind repeating it to the captain? I think he needs to know.'

'As long as I don't have to tell my dad about the spying. He'd be livid.'

'I think we can avoid that. And another thing — is the worry about your dad what's putting you off about your course? Are you concerned that if you leave him he'll find someone new? Is that what it's all about? You can tell me the truth.'

Lilly stared at her feet, and then a stream of tears filled her eyes. 'No. Yes. Maybe. I don't know. I don't want to leave him. But it's not just that. He wants me to be a lawyer because my mother was. I'm not interested in the studying or being a hero in court and reading through cases and debating. I prefer action. I want to go after the bad guys.'

Libby's guesses were confirmed, but

she kept that to herself.

'I want to be in law enforcement, not court law. What if I just want to be me?'

'Okay, we'll work on all that later. Can you go find your dad and check if it's okay for me to take you to see Captain Muldoon? Tell him you're coming to see the bridge if that helps?'

'I'll do it.' Lilly nodded.

'It's going to be okay. You may be more help in this inquiry than you even realise.'

'Oh my goodness! That's him. There's the man from yesterday!' Lilly said on a gasped rush and bolted upright.

Libby looked around sharply and she swiftly grasped Lilly's arm, seeing a man in ship's waiting uniform who stared daggers at her. He turned, sprinting down the deck and scattering shaken passengers in his wake. She watched him upend a trolley, frozen in shock. His was a face that jolted a briefly glanced memory from her port attack. She'd hardly seen her assailant, but his profile was striking enough.

'Stay there! Don't follow! Find your dad and stay away,' she yelled to Lilly.

Despite an ankle that began to throb as she started to run, Libby pursued, her pulse thundering. The man Lilly had identified was definitely the same person who'd mugged her.

She pushed all thoughts away and chased the perpetrator. He streaked ahead and burst through a set of doors with a loud bang. She couldn't guess his destination but was determined not to lose him. She ran flat out, her pumps skidding on the polished floor, losing her precious seconds. But when she shoved through the door, only a long corridor with a succession of doors on each side met her sight. She rapped on the first one and tried the handle, but it was locked. Libby cursed aloud. No footsteps sounded. Where had he gone?

Trying each door as she passed, Libby hurried to the end of the corridor, but saw no sign. Her heartbeat hammered out an echoing question, and she wished she hadn't been hampered by her injury. Why had he targeted her in Cartagena, anyway?

Libby knew she'd definitely recognise him again. Was Edna right, and they were all in danger? It caused unease to prickle up her spine.

One certainty remained. Drew needed Lilly's report as soon as they could get to him.

★ ★ ★

The news that a spate of passenger card fraud and a serious system hack had occurred during the last twenty-four hours did not sit well with Drew, and his gut churned; he'd encountered petty crime before, but nothing organised on this level.

He'd retired for the night, but couldn't sleep with his head full of worry. The joy of holding Libby was clouded by his ship in security meltdown crisis. The memory of a screaming Edna held a particularly vivid place in his recollections of this cruise's low points. Was he getting too caught up in affairs of the heart?

This morning's meeting had garnered his full attention. Around the meeting table, the faces had been drawn and grim.

'I think we have the upper hand,' Petra Martin, his on-board fraud adviser asserted.

Drew wished he shared that optimism. Passengers were being targeted and harmed.

But Petra was nothing if not thorough; she'd undertaken a back-up report to Zander's with spreadsheets and enough admin know-how. She must have been watching every passenger and staff member on CCTV. There was now a list of who had been in the crime scene's vicinity, and interviews were scheduled. They'd be able to speedily deal with the matter. But as yet last night's CCTV coverage had yielded nothing. It was almost as if an invisible thief had struck. With all these issues, anyone would think he didn't have a ship to sail as well.

A call to the bridge summoned him to intercept Libby and Lilly at the deck elevator. He left Hale in charge of wrapping up the meeting. 'What is it? You said urgent.' He sounded brusquer than he meant to.

Libby looked grim. 'Can we talk in your office? You know Lilly, I take it?'

Drew took her hand. 'Come through.'

Once in his office, Libby didn't mince words. 'Lilly thinks she overheard the thief making plans to strike. She followed him. She said he entered with a key card and so should have been visible on CCTV. She said he talked about rubies.'

Which confirmed, as they'd suspected in the meeting, that either their CCTV systems had been hacked or were being tampered with. Drew questioned the girl closely, drawing out her story, though she needed little prompting. She reported like a trained observer.

Lilly added, 'And Libby was awesome. We just saw the guy again outside the breakfast bar, and she ran after him like someone out of a movie.'

'No more chasing anyone. We need to keep you both safe. Thank you both for your reports. This gives us something concrete to work with. I'm serious on that instruction not to endanger yourselves.'

'We are safe,' Lilly said. 'It was so exciting when she ran after him . . .'

Drew summoned patience, especially when Libby said, 'I can take care of myself. And I still intend to go on a shore visit this afternoon.'

He took a deep breath and tamped down his anger at her stubborn refusal to see sense. 'I'm not sure we can risk that.'

Libby looked slapped down. 'Drew, we're on vacation. And as much as I take all this seriously and want to help you, do you really think keeping Lilly and me incarcerated aboard your ship will make a difference? Can you

169

guarantee we won't be at risk on board? No, you can't. Not without locking us in our rooms, and even that's questionable. We should be allowed to explore the port.'

Damn, but she was right. 'Is this what you're like in court?'

'I'm worse. Consider yourself warned.' She winked at him subtly.

Drew coughed to hide his response when he saw Lilly watching. She laughed. 'Woo, go Libby!' She peered through her lashes at him. 'Besides, my dad already said I could go.'

'Anyway,' Drew answered, unwilling to back down, 'how about I make arrangements for you and Lilly to take the excursion with a chaperone? I'm sure that way her father and I would be reassured. I'd also send out a security official for extra back-up. Don't want Zak getting mobbed either.'

'This must be what VIPs feel like,' said Libby.

'I'm worried he'll jump ship now he knows we're onto him,' Lilly said, many of the twists and turns from her recent crime reads jumping to mind.

'Which is why you're going to go through all staff pictures on our system now. I'll call Zander and Petra and have them refine the search by filtered characteristics to limit the number you view. Sound like a deal? I'd like him apprehended a.s.a.p.'

'You'll owe us,' Libby kidded. 'Of course we'll do it. We want him caught too.'

'My first real-life case,' said Lilly. 'I love it!'

'She wants to be a policewoman,' Libby explained. 'Keep that quiet, as her dad doesn't know yet. I think he'll have his work cut out trying to stop her.'

'So you don't want to be a lawyer? Has Libby put you off?' Drew said softly.

'No. I want to be the one who arrests the bad guys. Dad has no idea. And when he hears my plans to go into the police force when I'm ready to, he'll probably hit the roof. So I'm thinking of this as part of my pre-training.'

'Told you she was hot stuff,' said Libby.

Drew stood. 'Let me make calls. You've got an identity parade ahead of you. Even with a culled search, you could have a long morning. But it could just be a breakthrough. Good work, both of you.'

'Bring it on,' said Lilly. 'Nobody puts one over on us tough crime-buster girls.'

Libby eye-rolled, and Drew's heart soared when she smiled after he squeezed her hand. 'Let's do this!'

* * *

They found him: Carlos Cavale, a waiter who'd most recently taken to hiding in a storage closet. Security staff had combed every inch of the ship before docking, and he'd been apprehended without undue problems. The security team were thrilled at the development.

Libby made a positive identification from his staff pass photo on file. And this was independently backed up by Lilly, who'd witnessed the same man discuss the robbery. He'd been detained by the ship's security officials. So far no missing items or tangible evidence sealed his fate, but having a culprit found was a major step forward. Drew hoped it would pave the way to finding accomplices.

He walked taller, forcing himself to feel lighter. They could do this, and they would. And even though an accomplice was likely still at large, at least they'd made progress.

'Hi, Drew,' Nuala Delaney's voice grabbed him from his thoughts. 'What's up on board? A lot of extra security presence, I notice.'

The news was still confidential, so Drew segued seamlessly. 'New security protocols dry run.'

Nuala fell into step beside him, her red stilettos impossibly high for work. She might have been following him, but he'd been absorbed in his thoughts.

'You look like a man with a lot on your mind. It's been ages since we had a coffee.'

'Sorry, tied up for the foreseeable future. It's one of those days, but nothing that can't be dealt with.'

Nuala watched him intently, her shaped eyebrows raised. 'I hear through the ship whisper web that you have a new love interest. At first I thought it couldn't be, but now more people have remarked on it.'

Didn't he have enough with without personal probing? He had plenty of drama. So Nuala wouldn't be getting in on the script.

'It's called private life. And mine stays that way.'

'Heard there's been big important matters underway in your security briefings.'

'And how do you know about that?' Drew stopped in his tracks. 'Don't you have your hands full with normal duties?'

'Word gets around. You've always been of paramount interest to me, Drew. I don't know why you never give us a chance to develop our potential.'

'From what you've just said, it sounds more like staff listening at keyholes, and that bothers me. It's all highly confidential. I'd have thought you'd respect that. There have been concerns on other liners in the fleet, so we're only following protocols and setting up systems. It's an operational procedure initiated by head office.'

'Ah. As long as you have everything in hand, Captain. And I mean that in both professional terms and personal ones. You need to make sure her intentions are honest, by the way. I've seen the way she flirts with her actor friend — I'm only concerned about you. Some women prey on men for their own ends; surface over substance.' She stared at him longer and harder than he liked.

'I can look after my affairs well enough.'

'It saddens me that you never take up my offers to help bear your load. Even lawyers bend the rules. I just wouldn't like you to be used.'

Drew sighed deeply, then persisted, 'Libby's integrity is not up for discussion. With anyone. I'll get by without advice or intervention. And I don't have time to chat.' His tone compressed to blunt. 'I have somewhere to be. Excuse me.'

He left Nuala and her spiky heels, lacquered talons, and tainted allegations, minus some of his usual captain's courtesy; but her insinuations burned an acid hole in his mood. She'd brought up his past mistakes. Josie was Josie. She wasn't Libby, thankfully. Josie's failings in the loyalty department had become staff knowledge. But recalling her defection and throwing it in his face was uncalled for. She'd been prone to having her head turned. Bringing that up belittled Nuala's credibility as a friend or trusted work colleague. Nuala rubbed sea salt in an old, devastating wound. Staff had never been disrespectful before about Josie's affair. Using that knowledge against him now was low and cruel. But it told him Libby was a burr in Nuala's fur. He'd have to watch that.

Drew strode across the piazza to find the man he needed — a man who he'd got wrong but who'd redeemed himself consistently since.

'Captain, good to see you.' Zak wore his usual designer casuals. 'Fancy hitting the gym later?'

'Not today, my friend. Another time, though.'

'It's good to have your company there. But you look like a man on a mission today.'

'I need you to accompany Libby this afternoon. I don't want her on shore alone,' Drew stated.

'It's a hard job, but I guess I could. For you.' Zak grinned.

'I'm also sending back-up,' Drew told him softly. 'Nothing major, just some-one watching at a safe distance. No details, but things here are heating up. You know about the jewel theft on board, and Libby's mugger. I'd appreciate your help. Libby has a young friend to take with her today too. We think the culprit's now safely dealt with. But extra back-up won't hurt.'

'Wow. This feels like a film role. I'm intrigued,' Zak replied.

'I'll tell you all when I can.'

'The gym offer is open if you have any time. You could do with the endorphins.'

'I'll try. Thanks Zak.'

Just then he saw her walk towards them with Lilly, chattering and laughing to make his heart skip. She wore a shift dress in a cornflower-blue so stunning his mouth fell open, worn with coral-coloured sandals. Her hair looked soft and freshly showered, and she'd pushed her sunshades up on top of her head.

What if Nuala's right? You have it bad. But what if this time you're right and she's worth pursuing again?

'Zak will be your champion and chaperone today. Have a great day, all of you. You deserve it after all the help you've given me. And stay safe.'

Libby flashed him a smile. 'I'll bring you back something. That's a promise.'

And in only a couple of sentences, he was back on side and felt ridiculous for his distrust. Her expression erased the corruption of Nuala's poison.

'Enjoy the port.' Drew nodded and left. Unfortunately, when it came to unfaithful partners he'd been burned, scorched and left wary. And the result of that was an Achilles heel that wouldn't fade.

But time would prove his faith in one woman right, he hoped.

9

Libby, Lilly and Zak took a cab into the port of Ibiza on the famed white island, but Zak would not reveal what he had planned for their visit.

'He's being mysterious,' Libby teased to Lilly. 'Because the captain chose him, he's playing out a role at our expense.'

'I don't care,' said Lilly. 'Zak is cool. But what I want most is to spend the day with the security guard tagging us to see how surveillance really works. Have you noticed he has an earpiece and everything?' she admitted on a rushed whisper.

Libby drew in a breath. 'Listen, Lilly. I get that this trip is putting you in touch with what you really want to do, and I'm thrilled for you. But we know there's a real chance the waiter thief has an accomplice. If we're followed, we don't want the guard's presence rumbled, do we? Try not to watch him, and keep it lower key.'

Lilly looked chastened. 'But it's still super-cool.' She sneaked a glance at Barney the security official in the cab behind. 'I'm just so interested.'

'And here was me thinking you'd be the one with the kudos, Zak.'

'The tough guys always get the girls,' Zak answered, holding back a smile.

Libby had hoped that they could wander the old town centre, primarily because she was keen to buy something for Drew. She wanted to find something special as a token of her gratitude. But Zak had other plans. He escorted them toward a group tour standing beside a petite leader with a vibrant orange umbrella. 'I've booked a guided tour at the captain's suggestion; security think we should remain in public view,' he explained. 'Seemed a good way to get all the sights in quickly. Then we'll have time for a leisurely lunch.'

They wandered in the streets behind

their guide, their eyes slowly opened to the hidden gems of Ibiza's old town, founded by the Carthaginians around the sixth century B.C. and ruled in turn by the Romans, Arabs and Catalans. Evidence of those periods could be seen in the Dalt Vila, boasting many historical structures and relics. Libby became enthralled.

'The medieval walled city and its Gothic cathedral became a UNESCO World Heritage site in 1999,' Zak told her as if quoting straight from his guidebook.

'It's beautiful,' said Libby, meaning it.

'I thought Ibiza was all about music and partying,' Lilly quizzed.

'It's got much more going on than that,' Zak said. The town also proved an ideal place to explore, with trendy shops that Lilly enjoyed, interesting restaurants boasting menus that Libby couldn't decide between, and a growing number of luxury hotels and spas in its beautiful harbour. They roamed freely after they'd thanked their guide for the tour.

'We haven't time, but there are amazing beaches here too,' Zak mentioned. 'It's quite a romantic destination. And since food and love go hand in hand, how about lunch now, ladies?'

'Can we do a teeny bit of shopping? Or am I being a typical tourist?' Libby said. 'I need to get a small souvenir gift for a friend. And I did spot a great street nearby.'

'I know a restaurant near the craft places and antique shops. We'll lunch there so you can shop. I'll get us a table and you two can explore — as long as nobody goes solo.'

'I'd rather spend time video-interviewing Zak for my vlog,' Lilly stated. 'Think of all the cool points I'll get for that with my friends. They'll freak out when they see me and a movie idol together.'

'I think I can help with that after lunch,' said Zak. 'So maybe we should help Libby shop first to ensure we have time?' Zak pointed to a small quirky and crammed antique shop and pulled them inside. 'What kind of thing would your friend like, Lib?'

Libby was more confused than ever but decided to confide. 'It's for Drew. It's a gift that says we were friends years ago and messed up, but now we're better than before.'

Lilly interjected, 'I knew there was chemistry. He stares at her all the time. The electricity zings when you're together! I saw him squeeze her hand.'

'Lilly, we're friends, okay?' Libby said, feeling herself blush crimson.

'You know it's true,' her young friend giggled. 'Deny all you want. He's into you.'

Zak's grey eyes met Libby's and their gazes held. 'Our captain's a pretty special guy. I think I can help.' He seized her hand and she let him take the lead. After five minutes spent wandering and perusing, he pointed into a cabinet with a flourish. 'That's the kind of thing I was thinking . . . '

'Zak, you star!'

She'd never have thought of this herself. 'The lady wishes to see the magnifying glass, *por favor*?' The store owner opened the cabinet and presented it for inspection. The handle was ornate and carved in bone or some sort of pale wood. But something screamed 'antique keepsake for a man of the sea'. Didn't every captain need a magnifying glass for his travels, or just his desk? So what if it was all modern high-tech these days; this gift told of the romantic ways of the past.

'I'll take it,' said Libby. 'You should seriously think about being a personal shopper, Zak. Though I might get him deli treats, too, if we make it to the market in time.'

'We're not far from the restaurant. José, the manager, will oblige with better treats than the tourist deli. Leave that with me.'

'You're sure you can find the place?'

'I found your precious gift, didn't I?' Zak winked and linked arms with Libby and Lilly and smiled. 'I have two lovely ladies, a bodyguard and Ibiza at my disposal. Let's go and eat at the best place I know.'

*   *   *

The restaurant was a true find — boho and rustic, but with simple and great food stamped all over the menu.

'You know the chef here? And he's pretty famous, I gather,' Libby noted. 'I've read interviews in the past.'

'One of the best in Spain,' Zak confirmed, his eyes gleaming with the joy of being back in a favourite haunt and sharing the experience with friends.

'Oh wow, paella. My favourite,' said Lilly, diving in with her large serving spoon and giving them all generous helpings.

'And José makes it with a special twist. It's like no paella you've ever tasted. Or the best one in the world.' Zak grinned and filled up Libby's rioja glass. 'Libby, darling, I'm an actor. I observe and people-watch; it's how I get the fab roles and have a rep for being impeccable at what I do. So I do hope you don't mind me saying that I notice things. Like the way your pulse beats in your throat when you talk about Captain Muldoon or see him enter a room. Or with Lilly — the way her expression falls when she talks about her father, because she's hurting about her mother and so is he. It's so apparent that you love him beyond all else but are terrified of hurting him. So much so that neither of you can talk about it.'

The women gawped at each other. 'Is he always this deep?' asked Lilly.

'Zak is so gifted in so many ways it's almost criminal.'

'It's not a gift — just observations,' Zak explained. 'People always reveal their true feelings somehow. And I'm just saying it's there. With both of you, I see things about you; you probably don't even realise them yourself. I can recognise the deep feelings. But can either of you admit to them? That's the point I'm making.'

Libby and Lilly stalled their forks in front of their mouths, then stared at each other.

'It's true. I love my dad,' Lilly said softly. 'But he's shut it all out. Sometimes he shuts me out. Like with the study plan thing. He's building up an iron fortress for my future because his life took a wrong turn losing Mum. At first he hid in work, but now I want back in. Unfortunately, the things he wants me to do to please him aren't the right moves for me. How do I get his attention to make him see that?'

'Talk about it. He may just understand,' Zak said so calmly Libby thought it was like watching a seasoned and learned judge in court. Sometimes he took her breath away. 'Why haven't you told your father about this desire to join the police? I'd suggest that's as good as any place to start.'

'Because he'd freak out. He's a policeman who's risen through the ranks. And he's very protective of his only daughter, especially since Mum died in the car accident. There was a problem with her car brakes and she was driving on an icy night. It's like he blames himself for not having protected her. Sometimes I feel like I can't breathe. A life lived in fear is a life half-lived, after all.'

'He wants her to go into law in a different way, to become a lawyer,' Libby explained.

'Which I would be. At the business end of the job,' Lilly claimed staunchly.

'That's one way of looking at it,' said Zak, raising his eyebrows. 'So tell him. The sooner the better.'

'Would you talk to him with me? You make it all sound too easy.' Lilly went on, 'He thinks your show is amazing. He'd listen to you. You'd do it in a way I never could.'

'Me?' Zak looked like he'd just found out the world was flat and he was about to fall off the end of it.

'Maybe you could join us for dinner

and explain. You're the master at scripts,' she concluded. 'Please?'

'Said by such an appealing young woman, how can I help but be powerless to resist?'

'So you will? Fantastic.'

'I'll try. And together, we might just make him see your point of view.'

'You rock, Zak.' She leant over to kiss him.

'I know. I just wish all the women I liked share your view.'

'He's single and blue,' said Libby. 'Just broke up. And finding he often likes the wrong ones. Or the taken ones.'

'You deserve better,' Lilly told him, and high-fived him.

'I like your style.' Zak pointed his finger at Libby. 'Now it's your turn. You like our captain. Second only to how much he adores you — it's plain to see. So why not trust your instincts? Why do you keep tucking the secret deep? If it were me and I'd found 'the one', I'd be shouting it loud and staking my claim.'

'Um. Bad luck first time around?' Libby justified.

'That's not it. Because you hide from the attraction. I think you play the cool collected lawyer around Drew. Like you're scared to admit you care. How come?'

She knew her answer. It had been with her all her life. Fear of failure, fear of messing up. She'd been just the same with her career, though she'd stuck at it. But in affairs of the heart she had a self-fulfilling self-sabotage complex all the way. It had been easier to accept a 'friend-zone professional-equal' partner like David than risk heartache.

'You listening, Libby?' Zak probed.

'Yes. And you're right. It's easier to evade than risk losing the thing you want.'

Zak shook her head. 'It's all in your mind. You like him. It's heart-warming and adorable that you've met again. You're perfect together; as meant to be as seafood and rice, and wine and good company. And when it comes to you,

I'm already very protective, so Drew Muldoon is a deserving champion.'

'Stop buttering me up, Zak, and hyping Drew.'

'It's true. Do you know my fitness levels have improved since Drew began fitting me into his gym schedule? He could easily decline, but he's firm, fair and honest. Quite a man.'

Libby let out a long breath. 'He's married to his job and I mine. We split for a reason, and he's lost a partner too.'

'Do you still feel a spark?'

Just as Libby nodded her assent, a chair skidded back, screeching on the tiles as Lilly rose to standing, and the glasses wobbled on the table. 'Wait! No!' Lilly shouted, her attention now nailed by something over Zak's shoulder. 'It's them!'

'Who?' asked Zak, turning around and looked shaken.

Lilly's face was rolling thunder. 'It's only my father and that woman. And they're going into a jewellery store together. Why would they ever do that? If he's selling my mother's ring or buying her a new one, I'll go crazy.'

And with that she ran over the road before either of them could even think to try to stop her. But in three long strides, security pro Barney caught Lilly up and scooped her into his broad arms as if she were flotsam on lapping waves. It was a pretty nifty move. Moments later she was carried from the scene as if she'd never been there.

Of course the fact Lilly's legs were kicking and flying as she went belied that maybe she'd be a pretty tough act as a girl cop beneath the young-girl looks.

'Oh my, do you think she's okay?' Libby whispered.

'She's fine. Though I figure Barney's got his work cut out,' said Zak.

Barney went up a nearby alleyway, disappearing from sight, but it didn't matter as the man and woman who had got Lilly's attention were already inside the jewellery store.

'What should we do now?' Libby asked.

'What do you think we should do?' Zak said, being no help whatsoever.

'What do they do in films?'

'I can't remember. I usually have a script to follow, obviously. I'm the acting talent, not the creative genius.'

'Call Drew?' Libby suggested.

'I'd second that,' Zak concurred.

'Of course we've no idea what they're doing in there. How about you go inside?' Libby asked him.

Zak stared at her in mock horror. 'Me? The guy recognisable in most countries in the world for my acting kudos? How about you? You're a woman. Women buy jewellery all the time. Stick your sunglasses on and act enigmatic.'

Drew picked up the phone on three rings and Libby sighed with relief when he did. 'It's Libby. We've just seen a woman and Lilly's father disappear into a jewellery store in Ibiza. Lilly's fit to burst, though Barney's got her under

194

control, but she thought this behaviour was odd. Do I go in and lurk? I've no real reason to suspect them of anything other than the fact that there was a jewel theft on the ship. Could this be connected?'

'Stay back,' Drew commanded, his tone dark and clipped. 'Seriously, don't get involved. Leave well alone.'

'But my instinct is telling me to look inside. It is odd, isn't it? Shouldn't I peek, even just to find out what's happening for Lilly?'

'As you said, no reason to suspect them,' Drew said. 'You could do harm rather than good.'

'Okay. I'll see you later, then?'

'See you tonight. I hope Lilly calms down. Teen years are never easy, especially after what her family's suffered,' Drew concluded before hanging up.

But Libby couldn't stop thinking about the situation. Who was the woman with Lilly's father anyway? Or was Libby getting carried away on a dark cloud of suspicion; was this what happened when you knew there was a crime wave of covert activity on board a ship? It made you question everyone's moves. Libby checked her watch for available time and bit her lip.

'He said not to go, didn't he?' said Zak. 'I could hear him on the other end of the line. You need to listen to that voice, Libby. You have that look that worries me.'

'Really?' said Libby, already rising from her seat. 'But maybe I'm more like Lilly than is good for me. And what harm can it do? It feels like this has happened for a reason.'

'Libby, I've a feeling I'm going to regret this . . . '

'You can blame me. I sometimes go renegade. It happens.' Libby slid her shades down. 'Be back before you know I'm gone. I won't do anything bad. I'm only shopping.'

She was going in there to see what was afoot, and the captain didn't really have to know about it. This was her chance to find out about Lilly's mystery for herself.

★　★　★

Chiming bells sounded as Libby walked into the jewellery store. It was dark, with the only lights coming from the gleaming glass cabinets placed around the periphery. The store floor was deserted, but blinking cameras in the corners told her she was far from unseen. And suddenly Libby wondered if she had any business coming in here after a couple she didn't really know for an unknown goose chase, on a crazy impulse-led hunch.

The door at the back opened, and Libby smiled at the man behind the counter who bid her greeting in a fluent Spanish she could never hope to match. And something inside her clicked in to tell her to pretend to shop.

'I'm looking for a bracelet.' She gestured to her wrist, and then spied a cabinet containing a range of bangles and fine link bracelets ranging from gossamer chains to chunky bands. 'May I try some?'

The door opened again and Lilly's father, Mr. Lazlo, appeared. If he recognised her, he didn't show it, but Libby kept her gaze fixed on the cabinets. Her brief glance had shown a woman beside him with brunette hair in a tight chignon and bright red talons visible because she carried a black leather case.

Soon Libby was involved in trying on every wrist adornment available. Zak would be so proud of her acting. She saw Mr. Lazlo take out a document, and he and the man behind the counter perused it and discussed in English. She could hear them talk figures as if negotiating a deal.

'I have numerous pieces to sell. If you're interested, all are available. The pieces are in the ship's safe, but I understand these photographs will give a good indication. Ms. Delaney can bring the items in an hour.'

Was Mr. Lazlo really selling jewellery? Was this connected to the theft?

On the back wall of the shop was a dark door with only a handle and no window. It felt as if someone was back there watching. It was possibly a workroom or safe or storeroom, and maybe she imagined the scrutiny, but the hairs on her neck prickled. She tried to make her glances relaxed but felt primed, and hoped hard she didn't seem shifty.

'May I try the first one again?' Libby asked. 'I find it hard to choose.'

Time ticked by, and she was considering declining all the choices and turning tail to leave when she heard talking from behind the door that suggested others were in there.

'May I also try a ring? Ideally one that makes this a set with the fine chain?'

The door opened and a woman appeared. She carried two trays of new items. One held a showstopper stunning opal necklace, a doppelganger for the one she'd seen on Valerie Foster only days before. She also caught sight of a ring similar to one she'd seen before, its flower shape large and imposing. As Libby's mind raced, the jeweller moved to the cabinet to assist her and presented a number of other trays. Alarm bells sounded like klaxons as Libby's pulse beat in earnest.

Mr. Lazlo shook hands with the man and tucked his written information away, then Lazlo and the woman rose. Libby turned her head to avoid recognition, though she hadn't met the man often so he'd be excused for not knowing her.

'Just what I was after. Can you gift wrap?' Libby asked. She'd never in her life made a faster, less interested choice of jewellery. But if she got to the bottom of the conundrum, it would be worth it.

The couple left the store, and as her server disappeared to gift-wrap her purchases, Libby got out her phone with shaky hands. She snapped twice to take a photo of the ring in the cabinet, and then the opals. Her hand shook so badly she almost dropped her phone.

The jeweller returned with a perfectly wrapped gift bag, and Libby returned to Zak standing outside the restaurant. She was breathing hard when she reached him from the adrenaline rush alone. 'Sorry I didn't help pay for the bill. And sorry I spoiled lunch. But I think I have leads.'

'What leads, Sherlock? Find the hound of the Baskervilles?'

'It's not funny. Lilly's upset about her dad. Let's just say the captain needs to see my discoveries. And I don't mean the stuff in the gift wrap. I mean the pics on my phone.'

'I took a photograph on my phone of the couple leaving,' said Zak. 'This way you have some evidence. Though I'm still not sure I understand it. Do you?'

Libby threw her arms around the man who'd solved things for her twice already. 'Just please help me calm Lilly down. She needs our reassurance now. I don't have all the answers, but I'm glad I went on my hunches.'

Just then, Lilly and Barney returned. Barney shook his head as he placed Lilly at their feet. 'Sorry, miss. I didn't want to let you get into trouble on your own. And I believed you'd let the red mist take over. But you, Ms. Grant, should not have gone in there without my consent. You'll get me into all kinds of trouble.'

Red mist didn't describe Lilly's face, which was still thunderous. 'My dad has some explaining to do. What was he doing in there?'

'I don't know, but we'll soon find out,' Libby said softly. 'Rest assured, you'll discover what is happening soon.'

Zak's expression encouraged them both to summon fortitude. 'We're pushed for time now. And I got you some tapas treats from the restaurant for Drew. Let's get back to the ship and avoid cop chases and crime chasing from here on in if we possibly can.'

'Okay,' Libby said, taking Lilly's hand

and wishing she could offer magic answers she just didn't have yet.

10

Libby summoned Drew via the front desk, and he arranged to meet her at the deck seven elevator; this was becoming a habit.

Drew's surprise celebratory dinner for the Randalls should be the focus of later tonight, not suspicions and secret knowledge, so she had to deal with her findings fast. Waiting for escort to deck eight brought memories of that second day on board when she'd walked there with trepidation. How things had changed. Her heart pounded, knowing that the doors could open any minute and she'd see the tug of Drew's smile.

But today when the elevator doors opened, she wasn't ready for the stark, dark flash of displeasure in his eyes. 'My office. We need to talk,' he commanded.

Libby pulled herself together. She

ought not to get ahead of herself. 'I think that would be a good move.'

'After today, I'm wondering if you really are equipped to judge good sense at all.'

'What do you mean?'

'Not here.'

On deck eight he ushered her through to his office. A flat hand on the base of her back sent pulsing sparks up and down her spine. 'Do you realise the ripples your actions have caused? No. Because you disobeyed my orders. Involved yourself in a covert plan that was nearly wrecked because of you, and could have got yourself in trouble into the bargain.'

'Covert plan? Why didn't you — '

'Let me finish.' His tone was a riled one she'd never heard before. Libby stared at him. So tall and imposing, and now disappointed in her.

'I'm sorry. I didn't realise.'

'Clearly. Yet I specifically told you to stay away. Barney intervened to get Lilly out of harm's way. The last thing I needed was you jumping into the firing line.' Drew palmed his hair. His heavy, fast breathing relayed his anger.

'You should have been more specific,' she justified.

'Since when is 'leave well alone' not specific enough?'

But as mad as angry was, Drew kept her beside him by holding her hands in his. One hand crept around and rested on her lower back while the other tilted her chin up, causing live jolts throughout her bloodstream.

'I should be mad with you. You could have got hurt. And you could have blown our surveillance. I sent you and Lilly out with Zak and Barney hoping to keep you both occupied. Yet in spite of this, I've waited for this moment all day,' he murmured and stole a lingering kiss.

'Wow,' Libby breathed. 'But what was going on? I need to know.'

Drew said softly, 'Detective Inspector Lazlo proved our excursions manager has been guilty of theft and system fraud. Unbeknown to Lilly, her father has been working for us and is not in fact on vacation at all. She's here because his private life has got complicated since the loss of his wife.'

'Oh my! We'd better start at the beginning.' Libby raised her face to look at him, but Drew bent his head again to kiss her lips in an unexpected display of affection. 'Drew ... I'm sorry. Sorry if I got it wrong. But I've missed you,' she added, stroking his arms and enjoying his warm embrace. She meant it more than he knew. The feel of his presence so near to her was a comfort. His strong arms had the power to hold back the slings and arrows of any troubled world. How did he even manage that without a word or effort?

'And I you. But Detective Inspector Lazlo could have had his cover blown. He was on a covert assignment. The Fosters' jewels had just been sold on to the store. He was negotiating more safe theft. Both the store and Nuala Delaney had no idea Lazlo is undercover. She thinks he's a jewel collector. Lazlo had been working to gain Delaney's trust. I've found it unbearable keeping back secrets, but we had to bide our time until there was proof.'

Libby put her hand over her mouth. 'And his daughter thought he was having an affair!'

'He's been making links with Delaney, a woman who's been hacking our system on every voyage over the last year and a half. We had suspicions she was linked to minor fraud and theft but uncovered massive activity. Lazlo's been a plant to lure her in with his faked jewel sale. Today we coordinated with Ibiza police to seize the jewels and arrest the store owners and Nuala Delaney with an unexpected Libby Grant store visit.'

'Drew! I'm sorry.'

'If our officers hadn't swooped moments after you left, you might have jeopardised everything.'

The recognition sparked realisation, and Libby remembered the sirens she'd heard as they'd toured the streets as they walked back to the ship.

Drew said, 'It didn't go wrong, but it so very easily could have. And if anything had happened, I'd never have forgiven myself. You mustn't go against my instructions again.'

'Why didn't you tell me what was happening?'

'All was highly confidential.'

Not even Lazlo's own daughter, it seemed, Libby reflected. 'Lilly needs someone to tell her the truth. The girl's full of angst about imagined problems.'

'I'll make sure that Lazlo knows.'

'Why would someone take their daughter on such a mission?'

'She's quite a force to be reckoned with, I gather, when she wants something.'

'I think I'd picked up as much. Her looks belie her strength,' Libby admitted.

Drew wrapped his arms around her and Libby shivered with delayed shock. She snuggled against him.

'So the Fosters' jewels are recovered? And the fraud perpetrators are in custody?'

'Yes. A few loose ends still. But we're hoping our fraud issues are behind us.'

'And what about the Delaney woman?'

'Apprehended by Lazlo. We think she may have been behind your street attack.'

'Why on earth would she go after me?'

'She was working with Carlos and sent him after you. Our guess is she thinks you were undercover and working with the ship's management. Either that or she took against you for other reasons. She even told me herself I should be wary of you. Don't take it personally — she's a wily woman who's been trading stolen goods from cruise voyages for years. She's tracked down the wealthiest guests through system hacks and CCTV observation and accessed their accounts via data hacks. She had a lot of fingers in a great many pies, to the point that many of her victims hadn't realised they'd been defrauded. Quite a talent when it comes to cybercrime. She even had a gang of helpers who could mug guests in ports.'

The enormity of the situation hit Libby like an earthquake. To think Drew had been dealing with all this under the surface. And she and Lilly had been acting like they were in some adventure film. It was all so startling that she pulled back. 'Oh. Drew. I've been so stupid.'

'I wish I could have told you more. I'd never ever want to put you at risk, Libby. And please say nothing of this to anyone else yet. We aren't even telling the Fosters about the recovery of their jewels. We have a lot of ground to cover before we go public.' He smiled and then tenderly kissed her, and the earlier stress and tension totally left her. Drew had that power.

'I have something really nice for you,' Libby said, handing over the gift she'd bought before the day had taken a turn for the strange. It was wrapped in Spanish newspaper, though she'd secured it with a length of ribbon. 'To say thanks for last night. A memento.'

The smile Drew wore when he opened the paper could exceed the brightest moonlight. 'That's so fitting. Ibiza was on my maiden career cruise. Did you know that?'

'A lucky strike.' She smiled glad that the gift had special meaning. 'Actually, Zak helped me and he looked after me like a gentleman. He didn't want me to go into the jewellery store either.'

Drew promised, 'I'll use it every time I'll think of you and Zak causing mayhem. Kidding; I'll think of you. I have a special thank-you for Zak, but I'll keep that surprise for later. It's not one I can gift wrap.'

'Your surprises are starting to scare me, Captain.'

'Ditto. Maybe you'll listen to me more often,' he told her. 'Any chance I can kiss you again, given that I'll have to be on best behaviour later at the party I'm throwing for your friends — no touching. Boring or what?' He slid his hands around her waist and she melted into him. Then he gently kissed her. 'You make my day, you know that?'

'Kiss me like you mean that, Captain.'

Libby let herself seize these stalled moments, remembering that Zak had encouraged her to claim them for her own. She vowed to work hard to shake off the vibes that plagued her like the threat of a bad cold on the horizon. She put her unease down to uncovering more crime shocks than she'd been ready for.

*   *   *

Dressed to the nines in 'the dress that caused a mugging', Libby regarded her reflection. The glamour belied the dress's dubious past. It was palest pink, like a gorgeous confection, and it suited her hair and her make-up (done courtesy of Lilly, who'd proved herself quite a talent). Pretty white roses with stems splashed over palest pink silk in a fifties-styled creation that perfectly complemented her diva shoes. If she had a perfect vision of an outfit, this would be it.

For once, even her hair behaved itself. Maybe it was just the magic of being at sea. Whatever the cause, she'd snap it up and run with it — especially when she saw Drew nod approvingly and give that killer knock-out 'hand-some boy' grin as he approached in his full captain's uniform with his dress jacket. He strode into the bar, where they'd arranged to meet, and female heads turned. Libby's toes curled with anticipation.

'I get the joy of escorting you,' he said. 'Yay me.'

'Not every night I'm asked to dine with the captain.'

'Not every night I have such glamorous company.'

'I had to go the extra mile of course, for Edna and Walt's sake,' Libby answered, knowing she was blushing due to butterflies in her stomach, especially when he squeezed her hand. 'Actually, I need to have a word with you. Can we have a moment to talk before dinner?'

'I have the other guests to welcome. But five minutes *en route* is no problem.'

A tiny voice inside Libby squeaked its disappointment. He'd be busy with others all night. No clinking glasses over a romantic table setting. No chatting about old times. He was still at work.

'Advice for my trip to Barcelona. It's a place I've longed to go to, and I want to make the most of it. I wondered who'd be best to ask for tips on board. I want to cram in as much as possible. It's usually best to ask a seasoned visitor.'

Drew watched her levelly. 'Barcelona is your most anticipated port?'

'My aunt loved the place and wanted to take me. I want my visit to be special. My aunt should have been here with me and didn't make it. I promised her, and myself, that Barcelona will be special in her memory. Though Rome will be spectacular too, but first things first. Rome will be our final destination.'

'Leave it with me. I'm sure I can find you the best help there is.'

'Thanks, Drew. I appreciate it.'

And it was then that Libby realised what a different life she was leading to the old one she'd left behind. In the past, David would have dictated where and when they went. In a professional context, he'd taken the reins and extended that to her private life. Why had she let herself be cowed? But she knew the answer. She went along with it for fear of displeasing him or incurring his fierce temper. She'd become blinkered; blinded by his bias and his moods. What a fool she'd been. And now she was back, blinking into the light after a long time underground.

'You okay?' Drew asked, snapping

her back to the moment.

'Hungry. Looking forward to our meal.'

He linked his fingers in hers. 'Listen, Libby. I still want alone time with you. Hopefully you'll linger after dinner? I've arranged a surprise for the Randalls. Hope they like it. While you've been out exploring, I've allowed my team to make happy plans to impress my guests.'

'Oh, and solving major crimes. And wrapping up mysteries.'

'Man of all talents, that's me.' He took her hand in his and led her on.

★　★　★

Champagne flowed and the setting was filled with with sea-vista perfection when Drew met his guests in his officer's lounge for aperitifs. Tonight he wasn't due on the bridge after service. His usual orange juice was only heavily laced with ice, but even Antarctica couldn't chill the heat in his growing regard for his date.

When Sienna appeared with Hale, Libby's cry of exclamation thrilled him no end.

'You're having dinner too?' Libby enthused, hugging her new friend.

'You didn't think you could have all this high life without us?' Sienna gushed.

'They don't get out often,' Drew added over the brim of his glass.

Hale added to his friend, 'We should keep it that way. These ladies tend to draw a crowd. I saw the photos from Cartagena. They overtook the town centre.'

Sienna nodded. 'Captain's permission for a night off. Let me introduce you to Hale Hudson, my *numero uno* hubby, Libby. Isn't he lush?'

'She only has one husband,' Hale replied dryly. 'So the *numero uno* thing is a bit unnecessary.' He grasped Libby's hand and shook it.

'I've heard a lot about you already, Hale. Some of it good, actually,' Libby teased.

'Don't believe Sienna. I'm the ship

trouble-shooter here. My wife's the ship's troublemaker; Sienna's on a steep learning curve. I'm trying my best to train her. Tough job.'

'Cheek,' said Sienna, prodding her husband. 'I'll make him pay later.'

Drew stepped in to induce order. 'Can you tame the flirting down for one night?' He caught his best buddy's barely discernible wink in his direction, indicating he'd made a good choice about Libby.

'Valerie and Harry, great to see you. Your dress is lovely, Valerie,' Libby welcomed the Fosters, and Drew couldn't help noting that she was a perfect hostess. The kind he'd needed by his side so often before. A woman to be relied on.

Despite the theft tonight, Valerie wore a statement gold necklace with gleaming jewels that caught Libby's eye while Drew welcomed them and their drinks were served.

'I hope you're both recovered,' Libby said.

'Yes. And tonight I'm wearing a necklace I bought in the market for a few euros. You'd never know it from the bling. Maybe this is how I should go in future.' She motioned to the necklace.

'Good for you,' encouraged Libby.

'I lost a great many memory pieces in the theft. The insurance claim will be sizable.'

Knowing she was forbidden from revealing yet that there were hopes that the haul would be recovered, Libby kept her knowledge to herself.

The group was interrupted by Zak's arrival. The woman escorting him was dressed in ship's uniform and introduced as Janna Saunders, ship's staff officer.

Drew turned under the guise of picking up his drink and whispered, 'I think Zak will be pleased. She'd kill me for saying it, but she confided she's got a huge Zak crush.'

Zak grinned. 'Libby, meet Janna. Do you know she keeps all the staff in strict order? Apparently that means she has the awful task of doing the same thing with me. Do you think she stands a chance?' If appearances were to be trusted, Janna couldn't take her eyes off her dinner date.

Drew clapped his hands. 'Welcome, all. I'm so pleased you agreed to join me. Now excuse me while I fetch our VIP guests, who are presently in my office ignorant of what's afoot. Please feel free to welcome them with much fuss.'

The shrieking and shaking Edna displayed when she walked into the officer's lounge had Libby worrying for her health. She squealed and hugged her new-found friends in turn, gasping at the 'Happy Anniversary' banner behind them and bowled over by the fresh flower-bedecked tier cake in the corner. The ice sculpture of a swan from the ship's logo crest almost had her take a turn.

'We couldn't let your special anniversary go unnoticed. The initial idea was Libby's. The pleasure is all mine,' Drew told them as he raised his glass. 'To the Randalls. And matches with longevity. Happy anniversary to you both.'

Edna was speechless and then burst into tears.

'We're danged glad to be here, Captain,' Walt replied. 'This is some surprise.'

Drew smiled and continued, 'We'd like to pass on our compliments to you both with a special dinner, followed by a night in upgraded accommodation. And you both may stay there for the duration of your vacation.'

The assembled throng applauded. A door knock brought a ship's officer who presented a gasping Edna with a hamper and flowers.

'We're honoured,' Drew told her, 'that you chose to spend this special event with us. Let us repay the compliment.'

Edna had a river of wet tears behind her spec frames, and even Walt's surprise buttons were activated enough to silence him. But the grateful look Libby gave Drew was worth the earlier efforts in organising the evening at short notice with all his other pressing issues. And he felt his heart swell as she mouthed 'thank you'.

'Shall we eat?' He took Libby's hand. The party went forward to the private small dining room adjoining the executive kitchen that was used for VIP dinners. Drew's gaze met with Zak's in mutual acknowledgement. 'Our head chef's pulled all the stops out. And that promises a very memorable night.'

⋆ ⋆ ⋆

'Please stay a while,' Drew whispered after all their guests were replete with food and wine. His smile made her want to agree to any seafaring adventure he chose.

'For a short time,' Libby answered, trying to sound cool and watching as his satisfied guests returned to the passenger decks, vowing to go to the piano bar together. Libby crossed her fingers, hoping hard that Zak would continue in sobriety and that Janna was as into him as her behaviour suggested. She'd hung on his every aside, and it was clear that Zak too was smitten.

'I feel I've neglected you,' Drew confided after they'd gone. 'And you were my most important guest.'

'You haven't.'

'I hope you didn't mind the extra company. It seemed a good way to cover a number of issues. Unfortunately, the person who became a lowered priority was you.'

'I'm pleased for Edna and Walt. And it was lovely to have an evening all together.'

'Janna has the hots for Zak. She could barely speak, and that's unusual for her.'

Libby grinned at the match-making captain. 'I sense a good match.'

Drew feigned shining his nails on his lapel. 'I have skills.'

'Great to meet Hale with Sienna; I think of her as a good friend now.'

'Can I refill your glass?' he asked while he himself sipped ice water. 'You look stunning tonight. Couldn't take my eyes away.'

She brushed off the flattery. 'It's the dress that nearly made me late for the ship's departure.'

Drew linked his fingers in hers. 'Shall we go out onto the balcony? Ever been shown the moon by a sailor?'

Despite her initial unease, she couldn't help but laugh. 'Sounds like you're about to shove me overboard.'

She followed, intrigued to get some time solo with Drew. Maybe this would be a chance to air her heart's concerns. All through the meal, her thoughts had turned to Josie — had she been wined and dined in this manner? Had the captain's prior date always been at his side? Had she graced his arm at formal night?

'Sorry if I'm spoiling the moment, but I have to ask, Drew. You've never mentioned Josie. I feel if we don't talk about her, we're avoiding the elephant in the room. I feel a need to understand.'

He took her breath away when he silenced her chatter with a warm finger on her lips. 'Let's leave the elephants be, Lib. That particular one has no bearing on us. In fact it can't hold a candle to you.' He lowered his head to claim a kiss; one that lingered and swept her up in its potent momentum.

'Wow,' he breathed. 'That was the moment I've waited for. Big balcony scene. Shakespeare would be proud.'

She shook her head. 'You don't stay serious. But there are times we have to be.'

'I wanted to live the fantasy a bit.'

She worried she'd just thrown a bucket of ice water over his 'dream night' plan. But she couldn't evade things any longer. If they really did share a connection, they needed honesty — and confidences paved a way to understanding, didn't they?

'I sense we have to talk about it now. So you'd best sit down,' he told her solemnly.

11

The sea stilled to peaceful, its inky blackness offset by glittering moonlight overhead. Drew summoned the strength to see him through his frank reveal.

'Josie led me a merry dance. For a long time I had no clue, but she had other men under her spell on other cruise ships. I always knew she was a social butterfly; I just underestimated how busy she was. I was never quite sure where her pleasure pursuit would end.'

'I'm sorry, Drew. I'd no idea or I'd never have brought it up.'

He blew a long breath that came with the depth of his tension in revisiting past hurts. 'We split because I caught on that she was having an affair. But the hard part came when she was diagnosed; she stayed in denial for a while, then turned back to me. She claimed I was the only one she wanted around at a painful time. She shut everybody out, including friends and family. But she let me in and I couldn't forsake her in her hour of need. I helped her through her treatment. In the end, thanks to drugs, it was as peaceful as that sea is out there tonight.'

Libby squeezed his hand and placed her cheek against his chest. 'I'm sorry.'

'I don't even think she meant to hurt me. But the sea was more predictable than Josie Evans. And that didn't make for smooth relationship sailing. She was a big personality and loved to be socially gregarious. Unfortunately, she encouraged all the attention she got.'

Libby whispered, 'I shouldn't have asked.'

'You've shown me bright, happy hope again. And that's been wonderful. So the only hand I want is yours. The only relationship I want to talk about is us. I find being around you very soothing, like going back in time.'

Libby turned and Drew placed his

arm around her shoulders, enjoying her warmth. He knew she was sheltering from the breeze through the open doors and he acted as her harbour.

'The sea is my friend, my job and at times my enemy. But sometimes life's storms bring hard decisions that can be devastating. We're starting out and already I wouldn't have missed it.'

He watched her take a breath. 'You opened up to me, so you deserve the same. The last man in my life viewed me more as a possession to tame than a partner. I hid myself under strict rules and order. I thought I'd fall apart leaving him behind because he'd conditioned me to think that. He virtually ran my life by his rule book. So rushing into a new relationship is the last thing I need when I'm only finding myself again, Drew. I have to be honest.'

He stared at her for long seconds. 'Do you think I'd ever want to change you?'

'No. The trouble is,' she confided, 'I'm afraid. I've always played life carefully.' She shivered at the impact of the salty chill of a breeze that swept in. 'It feels out of character to be this impulsive so soon, though.'

'Libby. You must trust life to bring good things. You know my mother left me with my aunt as a kid so she could pursue my brother's musical future. Some might say she treated me like I was surplus to requirements. But it was the best thing that could have happened. My aunt was an amazing substitute mother, and my sea-captain uncle was my hero who moulded me in so many ways. My brother got the rough deal — a mother who constantly craved more. I got choices and learned responsibility. I was the lucky one who got a real life.'

Drew knew he'd never voiced these feelings before. Not out loud to anyone, nor even to his own aunt. Libby was now the holder of his deepest secrets. 'You were never a hex to me. You just thought we had an unlucky streak. You were everything I admired. Mistakes don't make you less — they make you human.'

Her gaze speared his and he let her tug him close, enjoying that she wanted to do so because he felt understood and wanted. He kissed her from the heart.

Drew whispered, 'You wanted a guide for Barcelona? I've arranged cover and I'm taking the day off. If you want me, I'm yours. Your day will be my pleasure. Sound okay?'

'Perfect.'

'I think we now understand each other a whole lot better. It's still workable if we want it to be.'

His fingers curled around her neck, pulling her into his kiss. Their mouths fused with fiery promise as her lips opened. She quivered against him and responded with hunger. He pulled her into his body, delighting in the way she trembled against him.

'Hale says I have it bad, and he can read me like a map. I'm offering to escort you in Barcelona primarily because it's one of my favourite cities.

I'd love to visit with you.'

'There's no one I'd rather have go with me.'

He smiled. 'It's formal night too. Want to go with me? If that's not pushing my luck too much?'

But an alarm drew them from their dreamy state too swiftly when Drew took out his phone. He closed his eyes before answering in curt replies. 'On-board emergency. Engine room issues. I have to go.'

'We'll find time again soon,' she whispered.

Drew smiled. 'You're getting my drift, my darling.'

He watched Libby slip away carrying her shoes, and wished he could forestall on work. Was a wish for a date without interruptions so very selfish, or was she hoping for the same?

* * *

A bouquet arrived at her cabin next morning just as Libby was headed for breakfast — hand-tied roses and lilies so fragrant the smell filled the room. The words on the card read *From me to you — with my love, Drew*. It caused euphoria to dance in her veins. She could hardly wait for Barcelona; only two days away. The city was now a special to-do because of her guide.

She touched her lips, knowing she blushed at the memory of his kisses. Then Libby thought of her friend at home, Chrissie and her engagement to Freddie. 'He completes me, Libby. That's as big and small as it gets. That's when you know,' she'd once told her.

The alarm on Libby's phone chimed out. The message from Zak read, *I'm so in love. Janna is divine. I've never felt this way.*

Hugging Zak's news and her own secrets tight, she grabbed her keys and went off to find out more.

⋆　⋆　⋆

With Drew tied up in ship's meetings and Libby engrossed in being more active on board, Barcelona arrived faster than she anticipated.

So on Barcelona port day Libby met Drew in the piazza. She'd filled up her bag ready for the day ahead. She carried every tourist essential in her bag, but with determination she left the e-reader behind. Today was not to be wasted and she wouldn't write any lists. She'd go with the moment. Today she would breathe every divine second in spontaneity. She was finally experiencing her dream.

12

'I'm in heaven here; I'll never want to leave!'

Libby's reactions tickled Drew and made him itch to up the ante of her experiences to encourage her enjoyment. His brain whizzed on where next and what else they could cram into their tour. But he didn't want to exhaust her either. They had a formal dinner tonight.

Barcelona's Las Ramblas market vibe was clearly like nothing Libby had ever imagined. He remembered his own first visit; an instant buzz for the senses. Drew simply sent her his encouraging smiles. 'You can't just look. You also have to taste.'

If only she knew the troubles he'd stalled back on the ship while he spent time with her idling like a tourist. He'd had to promise a lot of favours to get this precious day off ship. The ship's systems were still in disarray. The prior hacks had left a dark mark on smooth operations and brought glitches now in everything from the ship's ATM banking to the computer cash register system. And there had been another instance of fraud involving a customer transaction they denied could have happened, which was frankly worrying, as he thought they had the perpetrators in custody. Trouble with on-board financial transactions meant his tech staff were heads down and working hard. So he'd had to leave his staff working on resolving things, and that didn't sit well. Seeing Libby's joy was worth the effort, though, and Hale could summon him directly in moments if required.

Libby's hands were full of cakes from the market. She looked like the proverbial kid in the candy shop. 'You're going to have to find another adjective. You've used 'wow' too much already,' he said.

'I want to look at everything.'

'I knew you'd enjoy this.' Drew took the bagged cakes for her. 'This is Barcelona in the raw.' He had told her about the street performers who vied with stimulating stalls, foods and arty items. No surprise, then, that she wanted to linger while around them the enchantments were so vibrant. He wondered if her presence amplified the magic. Her face told him it did. 'Haven't you already bought enough?' he teased.

'No. I need souvenirs so I can relive all this when I'm miles away at home. I've travelled a long way to get here.'

In the end they bought a jar of marinated peppers, sweet oranges and a box of exquisite handmade chocolates. He got her tapenades as well as infused oils in fancy bottles. And when Libby hovered over colourful silk scarves that held her attention, Drew picked one out, the cobalt-blues like cornflowers mixed with sky. He paid and tied it around her neck.

'See, not so hard. You just go with the moment. Choose the one that speaks to you.'

He took her guidebook and pocketed it. 'There's so much to see still. I didn't fight for a day off for us to spend it all in the market.'

She stopped. 'You fought to get today off?'

He swiftly looked away and wished he hadn't been so free with the truth. 'I'm actually glad to escape.'

'What's up, Drew?' She shook her head. 'Don't tell if it's confidential. I'm not being nosey. I'm just concerned for you.'

'System errors and continuing on-board fraud. The staff are pressed to deal with it. Come on. Like I said, let's not waste the day,' he urged, and took her hand in his, determined to put the negative thoughts aside. This was turning into his most challenging voyage yet. God knew the crows of woe would be back on his shoulder soon enough.

* * *

Libby had known she'd love Barcelona, but had decided Florence and Rome would be the pinnacles of her trip. The wonders of Barcelona made her think she'd pre-empted. This city was a wonder she'd never get over.

'You told me you're a foodie, so first I'm scheduling off the tourist route stops you may like,' Drew told her.

These proved to be the Merca del Ninot and La Boqueria. Two of the city's food markets had her utterly at a loss for words with their variety and comprehensiveness — a true taste of Spain. Drew bought them both chocolate-covered strawberries on sticks as they left, and they walked like naughty children with stained faces.

'Leave it,' said Drew, winking. 'It suits you.'

She shook her head but laughed. 'Isn't it crazy that when we dated, I didn't know how to cook?' Libby felt herself blush at the memory of the dire meal that had made his mother so ill. 'When I dated David, he insisted I take classes. I went on courses and bought books. Now it's therapeutic and I love it. But I resented his orders for a while. I mean, how dare he dictate that I become a better cook to meet his standards?'

'What made you eventually realise that the relationship was flawed?' Drew asked.

'At first I thought he just wanted me to prove myself. But I suppose I was always a bit in awe of him. The wake-up call came when I got this.' Libby removed her cardigan to reveal a startling yet small and colourful tattoo on her inner arm. 'My aunt made a bucket list when she was diagnosed. We both agreed we'd get tattoos — a bit impulsive and wild, but we found an artist who did amazing, flattering watercolour images. So we opted for matching butterflies, and we did it together. I didn't tell David as I sensed he'd disapprove.'

'And did he?'

'I thought maybe when he saw it and heard my reasons he'd soften. But he was incensed at what he called 'my idiocy' and he rang around to book laser removal. The tattoo has special meaning — I realised it was important and I needed to leave him. He'd taken over control of my life and my choices and it had to stop.'

Drew shook his head, and his shock was clear in the intense way he watched her. 'Then between my controlling mother and your ex with issues, they did us both a favour. And for what it's worth, I love the gesture of the tattoo, and it suits you.'

'You have to say that now, don't you?'

'And I'll look forward to you cooking me a meal someday. As fantastic as ship's cuisine is, I long for simple home-made meals.'

She laughed out loud, liking that he'd turned it round in their favour.

Drew's hand tugged her into his arms to kiss her, in a Barcelona street as the sun beat down and life thrummed vibrantly around them. And nobody batted an eyelid.

'Gaudi's house next. If you think you've had a whirlwind of colour and creativity, this one will change you forever.'

* * *

In front of the majestic Font Màgica de Montjuïc fountain in Catalan so imprinted on her mind from books, Libby looked into Drew's eyes and told him her burning truth.

'I'm leaving work. I've decided. This cruise has helped me realise the law firm isn't where I want to be. I need to take a new path, and this is my crossroads.'

Drew studied her carefully, then nodded. 'Is this one of those movie-style life-changing moments? Do you want me to get them to turn on the fountain's lights and music?'

'Can captains do that?' She nudged

him. 'I'm serious. Who wouldn't have an epiphany here before the Magic Fountain? But I don't want to practise law anymore. I want to travel. A ten-day cruise doesn't even scratch the surface of all the sights and sounds I feel I need to experience to truly know I'm alive and living fully. I have a passion for it now and I don't want to stop. My aunt's life was cut off short. None of us can take tomorrow for granted, and I don't want to waste my life working and not following my heart.'

'Libby, I'm so glad you're finding the strength you need on this trip.'

'So am I. I'm determined to spend a year travelling.'

'I'm glad to be part of it too,' he confided, and their mouths touched once more.

The smell and sound and feel of the water echoed the blood in her veins and the certainty in her mind that held cleansing clarity. This was what she wanted. This feeling of bright opportunity and freedom. She'd never had vacations or chances to explore. Her focus had all been on work. Now she needed to take time out of life for this. She'd left David and could take the courage to leave work behind too. It really was *that* important.

'Being successful at it isn't enough. There are other things I can do later once I've travelled and dealt with my wanderlust. I'm thinking advocacy for those who need it most. I've worked with the big success stories via contract law work. I need to offset the balance and do what I can; first for me, to find out what I love most. Then for others.'

Drew tugged her close and pressed his lips to hers. He linked fingers and she'd never felt more at peace, more certain, more happy with her plans than at that very moment.

'You'll do that, I can see it — and you'll do it brilliantly,' he told her.

'I'll try. But what about us, Drew? I can't promise when I'm going off into the unknown. Yet I think meeting you again has made me see clearly for the first time in years.'

Drew put his arm around her shoulders. 'I don't want to let you slip through my fingers again. That first time was a mistake. But if I have to wait, then I will.'

She took her attention from the water and stared at him so hard he lifted up his sunshades, and she took off hers. 'You mean that?'

'I'm in love with you. And I promised I'd never fall again. So it's not said lightly.'

She laid her head against his chest. 'Is this holiday impulsivity, Drew?'

'We've done the fountain. And the epiphany. Now I've recited the *I love you whether you like it or not* speech. So let's have lunch? Somewhere quiet. Let's talk about stuff.' They kissed and Drew smiled down at her. 'You're not the only one who'd throw everything away for a glimpse of magic, Libby. Ever consider that one?'

This moment would live on forever in her mind's eye as a joyful perfection.

And the man surpassed the city, the location and the confessions they'd made.

This man made her world complete.

* * *

They located a tiny tapas bar that Drew said he'd found on an earlier trip. With quirky charm, it boasted a shaded outdoor courtyard with twining vines and delicious aromas from the kitchen. Libby's stomach growled.

'You order,' she told him. 'You've been here before. I trust you. I'm a veggie. And I'm starving. I've been to your captain's table and I know you're used to the best.'

He ordered in impressive Spanish, never faltering, and conversing with the waiter who clearly remembered him. He even treated her to fantastic rioja, and the waiter swiftly brought the carafe and olives and other nibbles to tempt them. They dined on divine tapas. Peppers, garlicky mushrooms.

Frittata. Even a veggie paella that was so gorgeous Libby knew she ate way too much. How often would she ever get the chance to revisit this sublime experience?

'Good?' Drew laughed, eating rustic bread and sipping his soda.

'Beyond heavenly. Thank you so much for taking the time to bring me here.'

'Libby.' He laid down his glass. 'It's time for cards on the table. I've been made an amazing job offer, but I intend to turn it down. It would mean relocating to the Far East — a high-end job, but it would bring huge changes. I'd prefer to see you regularly.'

'You should think carefully about such a big career boost, Drew.'

'It's a no-brainer. I don't think you ever realised that I loved you so much back in the day. I really didn't want to split up ten years ago. You railroaded me into the fact that it was such a wise, logical plan. You gave me irrefutable cause to think you were right.'

'I railroaded you?' She felt an uncomfortable twist in her stomach.

'Let's just say you were determined. I hear you say you want to travel — but I'm not ready to lose you yet. Maybe it's time for me to be more insistent.' Drew reached into his pocket and removed a box. 'Open it.'

She knew it was a ring box, and the feelings went crazy in her stomach. 'Drew . . . I'm not ready . . . '

'Just open it. It's not what you think. It's a promise ring. A pledge, if you like. As much from me to you. It tells you I want to be there for you.'

She opened the box. The ring's stone was pale pink set on a rose gold band.

'My aunt's ring. She passed it on to me and I remembered it when I saw you in that amazing dress of yours. I'd like you to wear it, starting tonight at the formal dinner. If you'll consider letting me date you.'

She gulped and knew her eyes widened. Shock spiralled and didn't sit particularly well there. Libby palmed her temples. 'Was I a fool in letting you go the first time? I don't want to make idle promises, but I feel like I can't walk away again. But I also want to travel. I'm . . . torn.'

'Then don't walk away. For your info, I think the food-poisoning meal was a fluke; but you were so upset, I knew you wouldn't listen. Seeing you again made me realise that no denying or getting past it works now. So I won't be taking any job that could get in the way of our potential, even if it is the big opportunity that's knocking. And if you want to hook up between travels, you'll know where I am, providing I still have a job once all the troubles with this voyage are dealt with.'

She reached out tentatively to take his hand across the table.

'Just think about it. Oh, and I'm sorry about losing your cat. I hadn't realised I'd be allergic. I didn't let her out on purpose; she somehow escaped. I've relived that morning way too often. I called every cat shelter I could find. I don't want to make mistakes again and I don't want to back down, Libby. Your love, however much you want to share, will sustain me.' He squeezed her hand, his eyes sparkling as her emotions swelled; but she wouldn't cry, she couldn't on such a day. 'Could you love me back?'

'There's no could, Drew. Try stopping me.'

A figure walked in through the door at a rushed pace, and Libby's jaw dropped when she recognised Maria.

'Please come, Drew, it's urgent. Hale has to go to hospital with Sienna; she's sick. We need you back but we couldn't get through on your phone.'

They stared at each other in open shock, then Libby blinked. Declarations had turned to dilemmas.

'Back to the ship,' Drew said, rising quickly. 'Duty calls again.'

13

'I'll come back to the ship too,' Libby stated, suddenly worried about Sienna and keen to assist in any way she could. Maria looked preoccupied and drawn beside her. 'I feel bad playing tourist while you're all coping with a crisis,' Libby admitted.

Drew interrupted, 'Finish your meal. The dessert hasn't arrived yet. We can book you a cab to take you back in an hour.'

When she caught the sparkle of her rose-pink ring gleaming in the sunlight, she realised she needn't ever feel alone. 'There will be time for memorable days in other ports. Won't there?'

'Count on it.'

After squeezing her hand, Drew swiftly returned to the ship; and after finishing the meal, she took comfort in ambling in the alleys off the restaurant they'd so enjoyed. Not that she needed anything; she simply drank in the sights.

Then trouble happened before she realised. One minute she walked perusing a leather goods stall, vaguely aware of the cathedral's distinctive spires in the distance. The next she was shoved so hard she lost balance, and in common with her prior incident all she could do was blame her own lack of foresight.

'Hey. Ouch!'

She fell back enough of a distance to land in the nearby road. Landing on her side, the impact knocked her face into the cobbles, and her leg jarred awkwardly on a paving stone. She shifted, and pain streaked through her like hot steel. This pain's knife-slice kept her captive while she lay still in the road, helpless.

An oncoming car bumper hurtled towards her. Car horns blared, adding to the mayhem, and her raw fear quadrupled. Libby braced for the impact, sure her life was about to end.

She sent up a prayer just as the vehicle screeched to a halt inches from her legs. Her fight-or-flight reflex had her gasping for air while her brain replayed the scene in slow motion. Searing pain made her dizzy and sick. Her bag was definitely gone now. Another mugger? Unlucky twice? Or foolish on all counts? What were the odds? She found herself feeling grateful that at least she still had Drew's ring. Did the world's criminal element have the hots for her taste in handbags?

'Señorita, *estás bien*?' Some nearby passers-by jumped to her aid, and Libby sensed a figure running off in the distance as she was carried bodily out of the road. Was he a cause?

The attack could have been so much worse, particularly if that car hadn't stopped in time. Fortunately the scenarios running through her brain hadn't happened. She was unhurt but for the leg injury making her senses spin. Her helpers tried to get her on her feet but she fell sharply back.

'I can't walk. Too painful!'

She'd been mugged, this time by a more determined thief. Her bag had been snatched in broad daylight while she'd been pushed so roughly that she was left disoriented and injured. And then the penny dropped. Did she have something that somebody wanted? Was her bag more important than the risk of injuring her in the process? Had someone tailed her while she'd been with Drew?

'Ow. Does anyone speak English? I need help returning to the ship.'

'Señorita?' Her friendly female Samaritan watched Libby oddly, talking Spanish that was more advanced than Libby could translate.

She pushed her bag-theft questions aside and concentrated on the next step. She had to stand and get back to normal. 'Can somebody get me into a cab? I'll get help on board the ship with the liner's medic.'

'Hospital?' said the woman. 'You go hospital.'

'No! Ship. I need to get back to the ship in port.'

Libby waited while those around her yelled in Spanish. She didn't understand the words of the kind woman helping her. The woman didn't understand her either, but Libby was grateful when a young man helped her to a nearby café. The owner brought her water and a seat, then summoned two helpers to carry her to a cab.

The leg wasn't bleeding, yet she suspected the damage was substantial. She could put no weight on or near it. A little beaten up she may be, but she was alive at least. All could be replaced, and she'd had no passport and limited money in her bag, having left her credit cards behind.

But Barcelona's bubble had burst. After thanking her helpers, she realised she'd never make it to the cathedral. And she vowed not to tell Drew. He had enough on his plate, and he should keep his fantasy intact even if hers had been bullied and muddied.

*   *   *

When she returned to the ship, it was a different one to that which she'd left. A lot of passengers queued at the reception area. Engineers worked on the ATMs in the piazza. Some of the shops had 'closed' signs across their doors. And all this she noticed from the arms of the burly steward who'd carried her from the gangway and placed her in a chair to wait for a wheelchair. She'd never felt more confused or ridiculous as she was whisked away to the medical room.

'You are going to have to go to hospital,' said someone nearby.

'What about the cruise?' Libby protested. 'I'm not leaving the ship.'

'You can catch us up. Maybe you'll be back in time for our departure, but you must go and get properly assessed,' said a helpful purser.

Drew might be in grave meetings about the mayhem aboard, but it didn't stop him rushing to find her. Libby felt worse knowing that Sienna was in greater danger and now she'd caused more problems. She was just leaving the sickbay when he found her. The ship's intensive gossip grapevine was quite something.

'You okay?' He looked drawn

'I am. It looks worse than it is. You've enough to worry about, so please go back and do what you need to do.'

'There's a bruise on your head and that leg looks nasty. I should never have left you alone. I think you may need hospital care.'

'You and everybody I meet. But what if I miss the ship, Drew?'

'Just get the x-rays you need.' He held her hand. 'I wish I could join you. Dr. Cara says she'll send an escort.'

'How's Sienna?'

'Appendicitis. She'll need urgent surgery. Apparently she's pleased, as they've been trying for a baby and she'd been quietly hoping she'd conceived, and this may be complications. It's definitely appendicitis.'

'I hope she's okay.'

'Keep me in the loop. If we have to, I'll get you transported to the ship some other way. Get all the care you need; that's way more important than ship's schedules.'

'I don't want to leave you.' She watched her ring through tear-filled eyes. She knew her voice shook with emotion. She was sad, scared, fed up, and deflated after so much joy. She watched the ring twinkle up at her, reminding her to sparkle through the gloom. 'I'll miss your formal night.'

'There will be others,' Drew said softly. 'Zak can go with you to hospital. He's already offered.'

He arrived later to find Libby scowling, utterly crestfallen at events. 'It's not so bad,' Zak crooned. 'You have me to help you.'

'You're such a crusader. Valiant and true. No wonder Janna is hooked.'

Zak grinned at her compliment, and while Libby waited to be transported she received a phone call from Sienna.

'Hale's told me you were mugged again.'

'Sienna — shouldn't you be in surgery?'

'They caved in to my many requests to call you. Are you okay?'

'Yes. But I fail to see why another thug went after me in Barcelona, attacking just after Drew left me.'

'Could be coincidence. Get well soon.'

'And how are you?'

'In a lot of pain, but the drugs are working! I'm not looking forward to surgery. A ship is always one big extended in-your-face-family, whether you like it or not. And what you and Drew share shines out when you're together. The sparks rival my Fire Mountain Goddess Dance costume. The one with the headdress that smokes. That makes you part of our pack, so we care.'

Deep down, Libby wished she could more easily tease apart her complex emotions. Lately she was all highs and lows, tears and confessions. 'Take care,

Sienna. I hope everything goes okay. Get someone to let me know.'

'Count on it. Talk to you again soon.' She hung up, praying for an easy op and recovery for Sienna.

'Here's your meds. Doctor Cara's orders,' Zak said without any comforting bedside manner, and handed her an enormous capsule and water. Libby knocked it back.

'Thanks, Zak. Looks like it's you and me with yet another mission ahead.'

★　★　★

Libby made it back to the ship before departure, her first ever broken ankle patched up. The boot on her foot was substantial, but at least it would be hidden beneath her gown.

Sienna wasn't so lucky. Hale returned without her, though he'd made promises she'd catch up by Portofino in two days' time if she was able. Surely her dancing duties would be curtailed indefinitely.

Formal night was officially underway, and Libby felt strangely at odds with the party spirit. Even Zak had taken the opportunity to dress in a tux. Libby imagined it was because he was definitely out to steal Janna's heart. Her grins when he approached communicated he'd nailed it.

'Don't hang back. You and Janna go and have a nice time,' she encouraged.

Libby's attention shifted when she caught a brief view of Drew nearing. He gave a welcome speech in the piazza and she kept her distance, mostly because she felt like a blimp with her crutches and booted foot. He sent her a smile that settled her mood and said more than words could.

Libby had chosen to wear her long peach chiffon dress because it covered her injury. Navigating a ship in chiffon with crutches was a challenge in its own right.

'Hey, Lib. Why are you hiding?' said a familiar voice.

It was Lilly. 'Great to see you.'

She hugged her. 'I heard about the mugging. Are you okay? Wish I'd been there. I'd have gone in hot pursuit and tracked him down.'

'I can just imagine you doing that. How's things with your dad?'

Lilly smiled. 'Amazing. We had it all out. He explained he couldn't tell me about the undercover role. That he kept meeting Nuala Delaney because she was a suspect. He couldn't believe I thought he had a girlfriend!'

Libby felt pleased that the girl had her worries smoothed out. 'Did you talk about the career stuff?'

'He's working on it. He doesn't want me to become a policewoman, but he's going to think it all over and he says it's my choice. Of course I think it's helped that Zak took him for a drink and has promised him a set visit during next season's filming. He'll come round. I've even told him he should start dating — through a reputable dating agency where they do matches on likes and interests. He deserves to meet somebody cute and sassy; a bit like you.'

Libby laughed aloud at that. 'Good for you! And good old Zak.' The pair looked over and caught sight of the man himself planting a heartfelt kiss on Janna. And Janna was kissing back with ferocity.

'I think she likes him,' Lilly confided.

'I think they're a match made in crazy,' Libby laughed. 'But it works. And love is a beautiful thing.'

'You're blue.'

'Yes. And I don't know why.' Libby nodded in agreement. 'Barcelona bombed. Maybe I hyped it too much.'

'Nice ring.'

'Isn't it? I should be happy.'

'I think if I'd been mugged twice in a week, I'd be down in the dumps too,' Lilly countered. 'Listen, my dad needs to have a word about your friends the Randalls. But he'll talk to you tomorrow. He wants you to keep a close eye at a discreet distance but will give you more info. I'll make myself scarce,' Lilly whispered. 'The big fella in white is heading over. I don't want to cramp your style. And I'd hate to get an up-close view of all the kissing, as nice as you both are. I mean, ewww! Gross. Janna and Zak are bad enough.'

Libby was about to insist there would be no kissing until she saw Drew's face was a mask of concern. And next thing she was in his arms and he had her close, and he was the one kissing her and leaving her in no doubt that it mattered that she'd been hurt and taken to hospital and he'd been stuck on the boat unable to help.

'You're okay,' he breathed as if that very fact sustained him through everything.

'Yes. I'm tired of assuring everyone,' she answered. And let him kiss her again.

*   *   *

Somehow she ended up in Drew's cabin that night. It wasn't the formal night she'd dreamed and fantasised about, but it was pretty unique and memorable.

She may not have indulged in bubbly due to pain meds intake, but that somehow made things more sharp and clear in her experience. She could distil all the special moments to treasure. So when the band moved exclusively to slow dances, and her foot meant she couldn't join in, Drew invited her to his deck for a coffee.

'Is that even allowed, Captain?'

'For you, given that you're injured, I'll pull rank. I'll find you a wheelchair and we'll scram.'

She laughed. 'Nobody knows I have a foot like an elephant under the dress. Are you sure you can handle that?'

'I've wanted to lure you into my captain's den since I first saw you trash your e-reader while wearing a fisherman's sweater.'

He spoke to a purser, who summoned a wheelchair; and once she was in it, he walked her slowly to the elevator and then to the officer's deck.

'You don't like formal nights do you?' she teased. 'I can tell.'

'Really?' He faked shifty eyes. 'Is it that obvious?'

'You play the charm offensive, but I can see the way your cheek pulls tight and you check your watch. You'd rather do the captain routine round a select table like you did with Walt and Edna.'

'Rumbled. I'd rather be up on the bridge — or alone with you. You always could work me out, Libby. I'm glad you're wearing my ring.'

'Me too.' She showed it off dramatically even though they were alone in the elevator.

They reached a corridor Libby had never been down before. 'Where are we headed?'

'My cabin. Do you think you can risk that? It's very nice. One of the best on board.'

'So you mean we pay all the high rates and you get the perks?'

'I just think you might like it enough

to stick around.' He smiled, then opened the door, and she knew instantly he was right. It was an emperor's room. 'Like it?'

'It'll do.'

'Coffee won't be long.' He closed the door and then stood against it, unbuttoning his formal jacket and then setting it on a hanger on his closet. He spoke softly, 'God knows we don't have enough time alone, and I just wanted to have you all to myself. But I won't pressure you; it's your decision. Tonight I was crazy with worry.'

She gulped for air. He had that kind of power. 'You know I'm tough as old boots.'

'You're mine. And I do care, deeply. Don't go. Just stay and talk. Keep me company.' But he kissed her in a way that suggested talking wasn't necessary.

'Then I won't. Just you . . . and me . . . and this foot. But I can ignore that if you can.'

He ruffled the end of her dress so it showed. 'I think I like it. And on you, everything's a hit,' he answered before he leaned in to kiss her breath straight away.

⋆   ⋆   ⋆

At four a.m. next morning Libby woke, startled by being in a strange bed with the annoying unfamiliar buzzing of a phone's ringtone nearby. The warm, heavy weight of Drew in bed beside soon reassured her, but in moments a tension returned to the man she'd finally spent precious time alone with — which had all been chaste, even though they'd slept together in an embrace on his bed. After all, her foot boot was hardly an aphrodisiac.

'I'll be right there,' she heard his soft clipped answer into his phone.

'Again?' It was an all-too-regular occurrence. She smoothed his back to wordlessly communicate her concern. 'Everything okay?'

'I've had better wake-up calls. Though being here with you does make up for it.' He forced a smile. 'Emergency on board.'

'Isn't it always? I'll go too.'

He shook his head and looked solemn. 'I think this one may be different, Libby. We're in serious circumstances. We'll talk later, and thanks for staying. I may be detained for a long time today.'

She rose carefully.

'I'll get somebody to help you with your chair back to your cabin.'

'What about your reputation?' she joked.

'They wouldn't dare. I'm a grown-up. With a big growl despite the charming captain disguise.'

She was now worried about him. She readied herself as quickly as her foot would allow, then they lingered for a final kiss before they both departed, a knock on the door indicating that help had arrived.

'It's like whenever we get together, you're always summoned away. I think you're owed a holiday.'

'You've no idea how much I want one with you. After this trip I'll need a break. I only worry that I might not have a job to go back to if things don't work out faster than they have so far.' And she saw solemn dread in his eyes that chilled her.

14

Walt Randall's face told of a sleepless night and a head full of worry when Libby found him on deck alone after breakfast. She could tell he didn't want to talk, but she didn't give him room for escape or other options.

'Walt, are you okay?'

'Says the girl with the limp and the painful ankle. More to the point, are you okay?'

'I'll live; it only needs rest. The boot's a bit of a pain, but liveable.' She'd had a very deep sleep thanks to the drugs. Her only hope was she hadn't snored like an engine with blocked tubes in front of Drew. If she had, he'd been too gentlemanly to comment. 'No Edna today?'

Walt sniffed with a definite shifty air. His gaze wouldn't quite meet hers directly. 'Libby, we're in a fix.' He looked over his shoulder like a man on the run. 'Edna mustn't catch me talking to you. She's forbade me to go near you. But I just need your take on things. In your legal experience, have you ever encountered people who've become stupidly involved in the fraud of others?'

'What is this, Walt? Don't try and gild the lily.'

'I've been an old fool. We both have, only Edna would never admit it. She still thinks she's doing the right thing. I'm only telling you because I don't know what else to do.' He took off his baseball hat and scratched the back of his head. His expression told of weary confusion.

Libby's mind did hurdles on what was afoot; Walt didn't cry wolf, so something must be up to warrant these confidences. 'Start at the beginning and we'll go from there. And I won't be running to Edna. I don't go off half-cocked, but I need full, honest details. So, you going to tell me? You trust me, yes?'

'Yes,' Walt answered. 'It's bad enough now that I have no choice.'

Libby's heart shuddered with concern for her elderly friend.

Walt's voice waivered. 'I've been stupid. Plain and simple answer. We took someone at their word and trusted what they told us. We thought they had our interests at heart. Help with investments, they said. We'd triple our outlay, they promised, and at first it really worked. We should never have gone there. I can't believe I'm telling you this or that we did it . . . ' The old man's eyes filled with tears.

Libby removed her tissues from her pocket and handed him one. 'Listen, I'm your pal. I've made mistakes in life myself — who hasn't? Do you know, I once went out with the most amazing guy and I convinced myself he could do better, so I ended it. Big mistake. So don't miss details. I'm a lawyer, which means I first gather all the facts and try to find solutions. Without judging.'

'It started out like a throwaway

comment,' he told her. 'They said they'd made a bundle on investments, and so could we. Edna was keen. We took a bad hit financially a few years back and aren't as rich as we were once. But Edna inherited a lot of collectibles from her elderly and wealthy great-aunt, specifically jewellery. We knew we had collateral, either to sell or insure. I had no reason not to believe them when they asked to get us specialist advice. They wanted to see our pieces. They were always most interested in Edna's great-aunt's jewels.'

Libby already felt her stomach take a rollercoaster dive. 'Walt, who's doing this?'

He stayed mute, then quietly confided. 'Harry and Valerie. They're very convincing.'

'The Fosters?' Libby tried not to show the pulsing shock she was feeling.

'We met them on a prior cruise and they promised great financial advisers to make money on investments. When they found out Edna has a fortune in collectibles, they made calls and showed us projections. We explained we were low in cash reserves but high on inherited wealth. They talked about experts who'd advise us for a fee, so we paid them. Said their interest was more in the historic value than the money. They offered to use jewellery in lieu of cash.'

'They must have given a good case for you to believe them.'

Walt sniffed and looked angry. 'They made us an offer for their financial adviser to multiply my savings in a new internet venture. Last year we took the plunge and signed up. So far the info they sent us told we were making a profit. Only on this cruise it's changed. They said they needed a double stake. That markets had fallen and we'd risk losing out unless we could double our initial sum. We told them we couldn't, so they said we'd have to sell some jewels.'

'Double? Walt, how deep are you into this?'

His gaze drilled hers. 'Last cruise they took five thousand dollars. They said their adviser would easily get our savings back on track. This trip they want ten thousand minimum. Edna's all for selling her rubies; it's me who has reservations. And most especially because now I've discovered that Edna secretly brought the necklace to show them. I found it in the cabin. I'm worried she's meeting the Fosters in secret and being duped by their tales and encouragements.'

'Do you think there's any chance they could be involved with someone called Nuala Delaney on board the ship?' Libby tried to stay calm. She knew enough from her work to know these kind of stories happened; opportunists looked for victims to groom. Then once they had their trust, they struck deep. The rubies would only be the start of the haul. But Libby couldn't reveal all her knowledge or suspicions quite yet. Even to the Randalls.

'I did overhear Valerie mention a

Nuala. It sounded like a very terse phone call; Val was irritable that day and took to her room. Harry told us she'd taken a headache, but she'd seemed fine before.'

'Does Edna still have her jewellery?'

'Hidden it back in our cabin in a chair.'

Libby felt a glimmer of hope. 'And has she made any arrangements with them?'

Walt shrugged. 'I know we said we'd meet for lunch in Monaco. Noon at L'Escargot Rouge. It's some special place the Fosters know and have been before. Said they wanted to treat us after the captain's meal.'

Libby nodded full of conviction. 'Go, and don't arouse suspicion. Stick to Edna like glue. I can get back up to watch their moves. Can you keep me updated if plans change?'

'Sure. If it isn't too late.' Walt still looked so frail and desperate. 'I've tried saying no and their tone has become insistent. I don't like it at all, Libby.'

'Do you mind if I alert the ship's security and the necessary authorities?'

Walt shook his head. Libby caught a waft of his familiar old-fashioned shaving soap and her heart wobbled. 'Tell them your old friend's an idiot who's past his sell-by date,' he said.

'You came to me in time, didn't you?' But inside her emotions spiralled. She loved Walt dearly and hated to see this epic fail laid bare, and felt as if she'd witnessed it unwittingly. Libby worked hard to keep her voice even. The battling currents inside her were so turbulent it was hard to keep neutral. 'We'll work it out.'

The Fosters might just be random opportunists out to defraud an old naive couple. But it could be much more. They could be the final link in the ship's unexplained fraud fiasco. 'Keep the jewels from Edna.' She took off her Ibiza bracelet and necklace and handed them to him. 'Put these in her bag in the storage pocket. Have you already parted with more money?'

278

Walt stared shook his head. 'No. The problems with the on-board bank mean Edna's been nagging for days.'

'For now don't give in to their demands, but stick to your arrangements. I'll get back-up and the right people on board to help.'

Watery blue eyes stared back at her in shame. 'I'm sorry, Libby. We've been fools.'

'You're telling me now, and for that we must be grateful. We'll have to move fast.'

Walt's freckled fingers shook with exertion, and Libby reached out to cover his hand. His were cold. 'You've got me on board. And I intend to make them pay.'

Libby saw moisture pool again in the corner of the old man's eyes, and it made her so mad she could happily have strangled Valerie Foster with her bad-taste jewellery. She firmed her resolve. 'Pass me my crutches. It's time I put my proficiency with them to the test.'

'You sure you're up to this, Libby honey?'

'We have something in our corner they don't, and he's the guy who runs the ship. And he's all fired up to solve some problems he's had with criminals on board. I'll tell him what's happened and make sure the Fosters are called to account.'

* * *

'My hands are tied. I can't help right now.' Drew felt her stare at him like he'd just announced a wish to move to the moon and set up a moonwalk academy. Right now that felt like an attractive career move.

Drew stared at the woman he loved and told her to trust him, but he couldn't give her details or a single moment longer of his time. He already had two top tech teams on his ship trying everything to patch things up and somehow miracle-work the banking system better. Passengers were irate.

They'd resorted to manual systems on most cash registers.

Libby's brow furrowed with frustration at him. 'But it's important. Walt's in crisis. You have to give me five minutes to explain the whole story to you. The Fosters could be linked to the on-board fraud. They've certainly been defrauding the Randalls.'

Drew palmed the back of his head. 'The best I can suggest is you speak to Lazlo. The ship's systems are haywire. We're working flat out to find a cause. If I don't get this cracked, the ship won't be allowed to sail tonight. It's not only an inconvenience for passengers, though many are angry and getting more so. It's becoming a danger too, as it could affect our safety systems. We may have to dock indefinitely. This is the most serious mix-up of my career. I can't afford to spare any other issue any time.'

'I just think if you heard the full details about what I think is going on, you'd agree — '

'No Libby. You aren't listening. You just don't get it. I can't and won't help on this. Work with security, please.' He saw the hurt spark in her eyes and wished it could be different, especially when she bit her lip and looked slapped down.

She narrowed her gaze at him and her raw hurt showed in her face. 'Why don't you want to listen? I thought you'd understand.'

'Don't be like that. It's not as easy as that.'

'I'm not being like anything.' She whirled away from him, though then unsteadily rocked on her new booted ankle. He reached to catch her.

'Hey . . . '

'Don't touch me, Drew. I counted on you for action. I thought you'd be sure to respond.'

Drew sighed deeply. 'Did Detective Inspector Lazlo get to speak to you?'

She pulled a face and rolled her eyes. 'Not yet. Why?'

'He's asking that you don't leave the

ship without a chaperone, for your own safety. The thug who pushed you in Barcelona was never apprehended. Ideally, security presence is wise during the rest of this trip.'

'Nice line in vacations you run here.'

'Libby, don't be flippant. I'm thinking of you. Until we're convinced that the fraud has been clamped down on, we don't want to take risks. Detective Lazlo will accompany you anywhere you want to go. Non-negotiable.'

And that's when her expression changed. She stiffened. 'Now you're giving me a police baby-sitter? Telling me what to do?'

His tone was terser than he'd have chosen it to be. 'I'm thinking of your safety.'

'Do I have a choice? Are you asking me or telling me?'

'I'm telling you. And if you're going to be difficult about it, I'd prefer you stayed on the ship.'

'There's always good reasons with you, Drew. Too many good reasons. Yet you're always the boss. Don't worry, I'll do exactly as you say. But I won't sit back and let Walt go through untold anguish because you're too busy to listen.'

'Libby . . . '

She jumped back as if burned by a spark. 'How can you cast aside my views so dismissively?'

His phone rang again. He had it in his hand but didn't answer. 'I have to go.'

'Why won't you listen?'

'I'm making a judgement call right now in the priority league. You'll have to work with security. Please.'

'I've always gone out for justice and seeking truth.'

'You're a lawyer who is on vacation. And I'm also annoyed by the fact you're supposed to be resting but instead you're hobbling about the deck.'

But she turned and left him looking so perplexed and puzzled that many passengers were watching him oddly.

His fingers balled into fists at his side. He'd never felt so impotent in his life. If he ever believed in hexes, and he most certainly didn't, he'd figure this one was their most potent. Drew itched to shout after her.

But already Petra was bearing down on him. Her glare telling him more than words could. 'The data systems have blacked out, sir. We've been hacked. A virus is gradually eating away at our data day by day. All systems are irretrievable, but the biggest worry is that all our data may have been extracted. Cards, names, accounts, private information. We may have to get a new ship to transfer all the passengers to tonight, or cancel. It would mean a ship full of very unhappy guests. PR disaster.'

He'd been commanded to make the ship's system issue top priority. This was to be the culmination of six months' work on high-level fraud to the SS Oceana Cruises Inc. fleet. He couldn't risk letting Libby upend this critical assignment's success.

And the thing he most wanted was to run after her and be the hero for her friends.

Despite all his efforts, the worst blow-up of Drew Muldoon's career had happened after all.

★   ★   ★

Libby walked with firmer strides than was probably wise, given her injured ankle. She could not override the very real threat for her friends. They had an hour to get to the restaurant before Walt, Edna and the Fosters, but she needed to do so without alerting suspicion. No time to consult with shipboard security, even if they didn't have a crisis already facing them. She decided she'd have to pursue answers on her own — just as Zak appeared from around the corner.

'Zak. You free? It's urgent.'

'Haven't I heard this somewhere before? Always free for you.'

'Can you come with me to Monte Carlo? We have a mission impossible on our hands.'

She heard Zak groan. 'Don't you think you might just be getting my movie roles mixed up with real life here? I'm an *actor*. I do it for a living. It's pretence; not real. I don't usually go haring into situations and I don't even know how to fire a weapon. The ones I use in my current series is a broadsword or a bow and arrow.'

'No weapons needed. If I said I needed you more than I need anyone, would you help?'

He raised his eyebrows. 'You know I will.'

'Good.' She breathed easier. At least someone was on her side, even if Drew ran in the opposite direction. 'Meet me at the gangway in time for a shore trip to Monaco. We're going to go where angels and Drew Muldoon fear to tread. But if I had to pick a sidekick, I'd readily pick you.'

'I don't like the sound of this. But

I'm feeling a bit action-hero around the edges today. Janna will be impressed.'

Libby breathed deep and said with conviction, 'This time you've no choice. Walt and Edna need us!'

★ ★ ★

'We've got it, sir. Recovered and reloaded all the systems. It's a clever virus but we've stopped the rot.'

Drew almost couldn't believe the words from his I.T. consultant's mouth.

'All should begin to resume as normal shortly. It took all we had, but we've won through in the end. The virus planted by Nuala Delaney had gone out of control after she was detained. It took the final full shutdown to allow us into the correct the systems. It had to run its course.'

Drew added, 'Shame she didn't co-operate by alerting authorities so we could intercept it. It won't help her case any. But congratulations, gentlemen. I can't thank you enough. Please thank the team for me.'

'You're welcome, Captain.'

Drew let out a Herculean breath at the words down the line and replaced the receiver, but the phone rang again in its cradle.

'It's Darius. Any more thoughts?' asked Darius Benton, CEO from SeaScenic Cruises.

Drew wasn't so sure that if Darius had heard about the *Oceana Onyx* IT scramble, he'd be candidate number one for his precious new job. 'Confidential, but you should know that this trip has been sabotaged by fraud and cyber-crime. We're on top of it now, but still.' Maybe he was being so open because he was looking for reasons not to take the diamond-throne job in the career crown.

'I'm sure you dealt with it admirably. I'd want no better captain on my ships.'

Drew took in a frustrated breath to sustain him. Darius said he'd give him a week. So much for patient consideration. But then they were the most headline-grabbing, trailblazing cruise company in the business.

'I'm still giving it lots of careful thought,' Drew concluded. 'But I need more time. It's an amazing offer. It's also a very big life move.' Then again, why was he stalling when Libby and he were hanging by a thread?

'We can do a lot of good for each other. Imagine Vietnam, or the unchartered trails in China. The secluded paradise nooks of Bali. VIP clients. A top-spec smaller craft to find the hidden unchartered gem destinations.'

'Darius, you don't need to sell it. It's the job of a lifetime.'

'So why the caution?'

'Bigger picture. A fledgling relationship. Meaning if I go with you, a door will close. And it's a door that means everything to me.'

'We're planning a European departure port. Life can still go on. Bring her for your maiden voyage and sell it that way.'

'I promise an answer when we dock

in Rome. Will that do?'

'The offer won't stand for much longer. But you're still first choice. I'm counting on you to come out for Team SeaScenic.'

As Darius rang off, Drew ran his finger over the ornate magnifying glass that lay centre top of his organised desk. Like a touchstone, it held meaning.

And he'd hurt her. Taken a firm rule. Lost her trust. Had he pulled rank like her past ex?

The woman who meant so much and had given him hope had his head in dark chaos. It irked that Libby hadn't rung him after their fight. He'd had no time to go and find her. Then Drew remembered feeling this way on another night at sea, when he'd felt sharp disbelief and heartfelt regret at the turn of the tide. Just like when he found out about Josie.

He'd seen Josie that night at the bar with the ship's entertainment manager, deep in conversation then laughing at his jokes. He'd proved quite the performer in all ways. Drew hadn't thought twice it about until he'd found Josie and Dirk again later, cuddling then kissing passionately in a dark corner of the stage, clothes in disarray.

Sighing deeply, Drew took the magnifying glass and shut it safely in his drawer. Redialling Libby's mobile number, he again got no answer. Thank God he'd told her not to go from the ship unescorted. That, at least, was something on his side.

He strode to his office door just as Detective Inspector Lazlo arrived. 'Libby Grant and Zak Nazar have been spotted on CCTV leaving for Monte Carlo. I'd left security instructions to detain them but they slipped by. The Fosters and the Randalls are heading for the restaurant as planned.'

'And why aren't you going after them?' Drew asked, panic slicing inside him so that his breathing ramped.

'We've enough police on the ground down there to handle it. The Fosters will be detained when they try to force the Randalls to give them what they want. The trap is set.'

'I'm still deeply uneasy that the Randalls are so mixed up in this. It's dangerous. The Fosters are the last link in the ship's fraud, and we know they intend to take off today. What if Libby endangers herself?'

'She won't get near.'

'You're sure? What about the Randalls?'

'The plan is watertight, Captain Muldoon. They'll be intercepted swiftly.'

Drew was a sea captain, not a trained policeman. But he knew full well that there was no such thing as watertight. No matter how smart you thought you'd been, the unthinkable could still occur. When it came to unpredictable high tides and deep waters, you could never be too prepared. Could he take a chance on letting Libby deal with that alone? The thought of her drowning in dire straits was unthinkable.

'I'm going down after her,' Drew

said, and called Hale on his mobile to take charge as he went full speed down the deck and summoned the elevator.

'She matters enough for you to take that risk?'

'Absolutely. You can come if you want, Lazlo. But either way, I'm going. I care too much about those involved to stay here.'

'Then I'm in too,' said Lazlo. 'And if the Fosters know what's good for them, they'll go quietly. I've had more than enough of their mayhem on this trip. We'll get them back here safely. Then it's over to you — to convince your lady you're the captain of her heart.'

15

For Libby, Monte Carlo had always held fairytale images of royal love. But today her mental images were torn to shreds and cast aside.

'Come on, can't we go any faster?' Libby clutched Zak's hand. She hobbled at speed down the gangway to bag one of the taxis waiting in port. She'd barely had time to register memorable architecture and a beautiful harbour setting, as no time could be lost. 'I wish my ankle didn't hold us back like this,' she complained. 'And I wish I could come back here again and do this once the panic's over.'

'Listen, we're way ahead of the Fosters; they're still back in the port. You know what Edna's like with her three bags and multiple sun hats. We'll be there in no time.'

Libby sighed and let herself believe

they could save the situation. 'I still have a bad feeling about all this. Why do the Fosters need to get them out of the ship anyway? Why not do this on board?'

'I have a feeling they've set up a nice escape plan, don't you?'

'Which makes me even crosser that Drew wouldn't listen. Then we could have swooped on them earlier.'

The perfection of the port's location between mountain and sea was not lost as they whizzed away. Monte Carlo still glittered around them like a prized jewel. But missing it would all be worth it if the Fosters could be stopped. She imagined in her mind's eye appearing in the restaurant and plainly telling them she knew what they planned. They could no longer keep asking the Randalls for money, and nor had they any claim on their possessions. She'd ask to see signed documents as their lawyer, nominated by Walt. She'd intervene to put their wishes over in no uncertain terms. And Zak would be there as added impetus and a key witness. He claimed that it was all for the TV cameras, but she knew he had plenty of physical presence. Certainly enough to intimidate the Fosters if need be.

Their car pulled up swiftly outside the restaurant Walt had first told her about. L'Escargot Rouge presented as a low-key place given its locale. The exterior might be painted scarlet, but the paint peeled. She noted what seemed to be a shabby chic interior with guttering candles on the tables. The Red Snail was in sharp contrast to Monaco's bright, pristine dazzle.

'Not exactly Valerie's style,' Libby murmured. It was the most un-Foster-like place she'd ever seen.

Zak paid the cab driver and helped her out. But her ankle jarred; she winced and fell back.

'You've done too much,' Zak told her. 'We shouldn't have pushed with this.'

'I'll be fine. It'll get rested soon

enough,' Libby countered. But she had to rest for a moment before trying again; he was right.

A man's face loomed against the car window, and before she could react he'd pushed Zak back into the cab and climbed into the front seat.

'Hey, what are you doing?'

Panic slid through Libby and she heard the man instruct the driver, 'Lock all the doors.' The man was young, tall, dressed in dark clothes. He could well be a gangster, and Libby rattled with the door lock to see if she could budge it.

'You can't do this,' Zak shouted, and grabbed the man's head from over the seat headrest.

'I'm police.'

The words made Zak sit back and remove his hands.

'You can't go in there. It's for your safety,' he said with a marked French accent. 'I urge you to vacate the area. I'm taking you back to port.'

Zak and Libby exchanged glances.

He may claim to be a good guy, but Libby wasn't so easily convinced. What if this was a ruse to ensnare them? 'We're meeting friends. It's just a restaurant.'

'Not possible; you leave now.'

'We have friends who are in danger,' Zak said firmly. 'We're trying to help.'

The man swiftly produced a police warrant badge and held it right under Libby's nose. 'That is not a suggestion, mademoiselle; it's a direct order. An exercise is underway. You must evacuate.'

'Your ID could be fake,' Libby answered.

'Libby,' Zak said, his face looking grave now, 'let's leave these guys to it . . . '

'But what about Walt? I can't just step back and leave.'

The next thing she knew, their taxi was in a street where milling police in uniform patrolled and a helicopter was visible hovering over the end of the street. Another policeman walked to the cab and pulled them out. Zak was pushed ahead with an arm up his back.

'You will be detained for your safety,' the policeman told them.

What was Walt mixed up in? And however would they survive this?

* * *

Libby and Zak hadn't noticed. Walt saw them in his peripheral vision as they were led away from their cab. But they were so intent on gaining the restaurant to help him and Edna that they were blind to their surroundings. They hadn't noticed that the Valerie stooge was in fact a man in a wig and Harry another imposter.

Walt knew they probably believed Edna was fussing again. She was, but much more low key than was usual; this time with due cause: a gun pressed into her spine to ensure her silence ensured she complied.

Walt wished he could have called Libby and tipped her off, but they'd taken his phone away. Their captors issued quiet orders. Neither Libby nor Zak twigged that his wife's silence was due to fear. Edna's dramatics had finally led to a sinister 'cry wolf' finale.

Walt knew Edna had tried to scream as he was being raised in his wheelchair into the taxi at gunpoint, but her voice was so frail it didn't carry. And she was so fraught with shakes it froze in her throat. Being petite, she was easy to bundle in, and they swiftly gagged her.

The Fosters were gone; they must have known they'd been rumbled after Delaney's departure and more security presence on board. Walt figured they'd worked out they were on borrowed time, so staying around for Edna's rubies was no longer the top concern.

They must have ordered their accomplice thugs to take care of them. Maybe steal the jewels and dump them, likely somewhere remote where they wouldn't be found for a while. If Walt knew anything of Valerie, it was that she was greedy enough not to let an opportunity go. He had it worked out now. Delaney and the Fosters had been only tentatively milking the cyber fraud of passenger data from their last voyages. This voyage was to be their ultimate coup, with a big payoff. Only IT glitches had always gone wrong; Libby had told him as much.

Nuala Delaney threatened to bail on the scam. Harry Foster had then used him and Edna as a short-term cash window. He'd used the money to placate Nuala to keep her on side. But when Delaney tried the scams again and system problems went rogue, she'd been caught red-handed. A stunt theft from their room made them appear convincing innocent victims. That was probably initiated by the Fosters themselves. They were as good at acting as Zak was.

'Put the weapons down,' sounded a voice through a loudspeaker just as Edna had been pushed in the car. Her screams came out, finally piercing the air and his heart. With much shouting, the assailants shut the doors hard, but already armed police swarmed in like beetles around a carcass.

The two ship's waiters who'd disguised themselves as the Fosters had, Walt realised, ironically always seemed attentive during service. Now he knew why they'd been so vigilant. Had they been weighing them up for the big strike? Walt had never let on his suspicions about his room door handle turning in the night. Edna would have freaked like crazy.

Two officers ran at the men, who hit pavement laying low. The whirling helicopter in the sky seemed to come from nowhere. Two bullets fired. But in seconds both men had their weapons kicked away.

While Edna sobbed, Walt hung his head in silent remorse and relief. He'd finally worked out a semblance version of the jigsaw of deception.

They weren't going to die yet. But

he'd worked it out much too late to get out of this without scars.

★　★　★

Lazlo and Drew didn't get further than deck seven when a voice sounded from behind. 'It's over.'

Harry Randall moved from the shadows into Drew's direct line of vision. 'You think you're clever. But you're as hapless as the company who made it possible to take over all the accounts. Our last five cruises have been funded by incompetence. And your customers.'

'Clever. Or are you?' Drew parried. 'You're still here. Not on a Monaco yacht living the life of Riley quite yet.'

Lazlo shot a warning glance. He saw Harry's jaw tick.

But Drew pushed anyway, 'Technically you're still on *my boat*. Under my jurisdiction. Must hit hard.'

'Yet I'm the one with the gun.'

They both saw the man's fingers flex over the trigger. 'But rest assured, we'll get away. With your compliance.' Harry stepped closer. 'You shouldn't have messed with our plan. You shouldn't have meddled with Nuala or getting the system fixed. We had it set for melt-down. Now things will get messy; your girl for starters. Always sticking her nose in. Typical lawyer. We tried to stop her but she's . . . rather determined.'

Drew's jaw clenched. 'There's an armed police guard outside. They'll keep her on the right side of the safety line now.'

'Maybe you should have been more concerned about your own safety, Captain? No police presence here, except him. Not that I'm impressed. Hardly top league.'

Lazlo ignored the insults. 'I was on to you. Softly, softly catchee monkey. You're here now. The IT systems are fixed. I've been informed that any major cash fraud will be invalid if attempted now. Until now you've really only chanced piecemeal sums. Hardly a retirement fund for someone with fine tastes. And that will all be refunded to victims in due course now we have the evidence.'

Drew saw the anger gleam in Harry's eyes. 'Ah, the precious Randalls. Everybody's darlings — or the ones you'd choose to avoid. Putting up with her deserved danger money. They're the ones you should be watching for. We'll soon have their jewels signed away to us.'

'Really?' said Lazlo. 'Can't you hear the helicopter?'

Harry's eyes shifted as he listened with a concentrated effort. 'You're bluffing. They're right now being taken somewhere quiet where nobody will hear the gunshots. The jewels are waiting; I really must get on.'

'I hope this was worth the stretch in prison. Attempted murder's a pretty hefty charge for a vacation final bill.'

'We don't intend to get caught.' Harry stepped forward. 'Now if you don't mind, we've a boat waiting. Escort me to it; we'd like to board. C'mon, Val.'

It was only then they noticed her cowering in tears in the corner.

'Getting you off my ship will be a pleasure.' Drew quashed the urge to use his martial arts skills to take the man down but instead saw the flicker of a wink from Lazlo.

They walked to the elevator, Harry Foster's gun hidden beneath his jacket. Valerie was pale-faced and tight-lipped. Drew sensed she was in this way above her window of tolerance, but her crazed husband was on a roll.

'I'll be happy to take you out . . . ' Drew said as the doors of the elevator closed and in two swift moves Lazlo lunged at Harry and Drew kicked hard at midpoint. But the gun didn't drop and Harry shot wildly, the bullet firing so loud it was like a bomb in the small enclosure.

And after the bullet knocked Drew to the floor of the elevator, Valerie Foster's screams sounded louder than the helicopter. Like they'd journeyed into the depths of hell.

It was way too long before Libby was allowed into the medical bay to see Drew. She felt as if her nerves had gone twenty-five rounds with impatience boxing her thoughts with knock-out blows.

He'd been shot at. In a confined space. By Harry Randall.

She held onto the fact that she'd also been told he survived thanks to his bullet-proof vest. He'd been wearing one, thank heavens. Though how and why, she badly needed to investigate. She felt like she'd watched a year's soap marathon in one sitting. And now her stress levels were maxed.

'You can come through now,' said Cara, the ship's doctor. 'Please try not to tire him.'

'Tire him? I'll go crazy with rage.'

Cara shook her head. 'I know you're kidding. Even then — give him time. It's a pretty shocking experience, being shot at. Even with the appropriate body armour. He's got some serious bruising and possibly a cracked rib.'

Libby peered around the side of the door and saw Drew lying on top of the sick bed. She immediately felt tears rise. Unbidden tears; she so didn't want to do this. But it was so emotionally draining. Hearing all the varied stories of the day had frankly wrecked her peace of mind. She'd already sobbed all over Lilly Lazlo once. The poor kid must think she was unstable.

'Hey,' Drew said softly.

'I haven't brought you chocolate. Or grapes.'

'It's okay. It's not like it was planned.'

'Not even funny,' Libby said on a rushed whisper. She approached the bed, scared to touch him, frightened to breathe as stress and fear flooded her system. This could have been so much worse! And where would she have turned if Drew had been hurt? Or worse?

'What if it had been somewhere the vest didn't cover?' she said.

309

'Look. If ifs and ands were pots and pans . . . '

'Drew, I'm serious. Why were you wearing the vest?'

'We had a suspicion things might get hairy. It was just a precaution.'

'Drew!'

'Libby, I'm fine. I'll have a bruise and a half and my head's not on straight yet, but I'm fine. Or I will be when you kiss me.'

'Are we still talking? I'm not sure we're at a place where kissing can happen. You pushed me out at a very important time. You wouldn't listen.'

'I told you not to leave the ship and you ignored me! Lib, I can't even begin to say sorry for the way I behaved. I had a million jostling priorities and I pushed out the wrong one. I'm sorry. I can't make amends, but I can promise you I'll never put you second again.'

'I've had that said to me before.' She bit her lip and held back the tears.

'Then I'll make sure I prove it. I can

only hope to earn your trust back. I'll make that my firm mission. Let me try. Do remember, I was trying to keep you safe.'

His look melted her resolve and she went forward, rushing to him, glad to be held in his arms and find him living and breathing with a heart that she loved with all of her own.

'If you need the whole story, speak to Lazlo. He has all the details. But we can finally lay this case to rest. All perpetrators in custody. All issues resolved. Well, nearly . . . I've something else to tell you. I need to disembark. They're bringing on a temp captain to replace me.'

Libby stared at him, not quite able to process what he'd just said, and not even wanting to go there to imagine what life would be like aboard this ship without him. 'Why?' she whispered.

'Because I'm wanted to assist with enquiries. And it's protocol for the company during an investigation. There's no reason to think that it won't all be dealt with in the minimum of time. Plus in their eyes I might be a liability. I've just been shot at. There's rather a lot of passengers on board relying on my steady hand. So I figure it's time to bow out for now.'

'Drew . . . I can't bear it . . . '

'You can and you will. Remember when we met? You wanted me gone. Hold on to that. But I will come back and find you. Trust in that. As long as we're talking again, I can deal with anything.'

She kissed him, wishing they hadn't had all this upset and trauma and fear and tension to tear up their precious time. Wishing she hadn't gone AWOL and off the handle and muddied their trust. Libby burst into tears for a fourth time that day.

'Come on, now. I love you. And I'll be sailing right back into your arms as soon as I'm fit.'

'If you don't, Drew Muldoon, trust on it — I'll come after you.'

'That I don't doubt — with Lilly and

312

Zak as your sidekicks. And I'd very much like to see it,' he answered.

⋆ ⋆ ⋆

'Come on, Lib. You're not concentrating again,' said Zak, watching her accusingly.

'I'm not in the mood for chess.'

'That's why he's winning?' said Janna. 'I'll see you two around later. Hey, Lib. Cheer up.' She leant over to kiss her man and Libby looked away as she lingered for a second peck. They were clearly crazy nuts about each other. So it was okay for Janna to say chin up, but she just couldn't.

Since the siege experience, they'd all been understandably quiet and low. The Randalls weren't the only ones who'd be glad when this trip was over; she knew how they felt. In fact many of the passengers had been shaken by events. Even though they'd all received notification of a sizeable refund from the company, it was hard to shake how serious things had been.

313

And lately Drew wasn't replying to her messages. She texted at least twice a day, but there had been no word. Maybe he'd just had time to wake up to their finite future?

'Stop moping. Your guy is going to be okay,' Zak assured her.

'It's not that. It's everything. This was supposed to be a dream trip, but it's had its share of nightmares.'

'Think on the positives,' Zak encouraged. 'You've met great friends. You helped save your friends from an awful plight. You met a great guy. If you're not going to cheer up, I'm going to have to start juggling champagne bottles to entertain you.'

'Um, I think we'll shelve that one permanently.'

'And my point is, you even showed me the error of my ways. You happened to fall deeply in love with a man who you're now worrying like crazy about. You need to trust in him. And trust in yourself. He'll be true to his word, Libby. Just because he can't be here doesn't mean he doesn't want to be.'

'I'm not so sure. We're just at the beginnings of things . . . '

Zak pulled a debonair smile. 'Wondering and worrying won't help. So let's act like we're on holiday and make like we know how to live. Fancy a cocktail? You *are* still on holiday. You were a wet blanket in Portofino, so have something nice to put the smile back on your face. How about a Fruity Flirtation?'

'Don't let Janna hear you say that.'

Zak widened his eyes reading the menu card. 'Ah . . . I think I know what to get you. A Sea Captain's Sangria.' He tossed the cocktail menu down and rose to order. 'I'll maybe just take a snap of you looking so sad and accidentally send it to the captain we both love so.'

'Don't you dare, Zak!'

'Then cheer up,' he answered. 'One cocktail coming. Watch out for the swell of your devoted heart.'

The journey from the port to Rome was longer than Libby had realised. And while she was glad to finally be going to the city she'd most longed to visit, there was something in her heart that stayed dark and dismayed.

Nothing had been the same since Drew's departure. She understood his reasons, and ship's protocols had to be obeyed, but her voyage had taken a turn for the bleaker.

Not that Hale wasn't an admirable replacement with the new officer posted to second him. And with Sienna back with them since Portofino, things had been boosted. But Drew's were hard shoes to fill. Despite trying to message him, he'd left texts unanswered. She'd attempted to call but it had rung out.

Libby realised she'd made assumptions about Drew's high-handedness. Was this a sign she'd never cope with a man's rules? Had David gouged a wound in her heart that even Drew could not rebuild? Maybe David had made her ultra-sensitive, but she had her reasons for her distrust. Could Drew see past this? She was sure of only one thing — his lack of contact communicated a step back. She'd taken this as far as removing the ring from her finger and storing it in its box in her bag.

Libby opened her guidebook, following the tour she'd booked and hoping to find enthusiasm for this special conclusion to her trip. The tour fittingly started at the Trevi Fountain, a landmark she'd often looked at online and in books. She stood marvelling at its detail and its splendour. And yet her mind kept returning to Barcelona and how different she'd felt there, with the man she loved with all her heart beside her and a future full of bright hope.

'What is it about you and fountains?' A familiar male voice said beside her. Drew's voice. A voice she'd never ever want to forget.

She turned to watch him with saucer-eyed wonder, then ran and threw her arms around his neck.

'Yes. It's not a hologram or a mirage. I'm here, just for you.'

The guide called over to them to ask them to be quiet as they were spoiling the enjoyment of other tourists, and Libby stood back, Drew guiding her by the arm.

'I've had spies tracking your movements,' he explained. 'As of this morning, interviews over and complete. I believe all parties have been charged. We wrapped things up nicely. Sorry about my phone. It chose a great time to die and I haven't replaced it.'

'Drew, how can you ever call getting shot at as nice?'

'That was a bit of a bolt from the blue. But thanks to a trusty detective I know, he'd sorted me out with armour.'

'Shame he couldn't have prepped me for the heart attack it caused me.'

He tugged her close and kissed her, covering her lips with his own and lingering over the gesture. 'I have a confession,' he whispered.

Libby shook her head. 'I don't think I can take more.'

With slow care, Drew watched her levelly as he rolled up his sleeve. There on his lower bicep was a sight that made her gasp in shock. The tattoo still boasted a red tinge and its clear cling-film cover to protect it.

'You didn't!' Libby gaped.

'You got me to thinking that many sailors do indeed have tattoos. And maybe it was time I took the plunge and got inked myself.'

'You're a ship's captain, not a bored pirate on shore leave.'

'I liked your subtle, special tattoo. Read it, Libby. It should give you a message loud and clear; just read it.'

The intricate script on his skin read *Ha detto sì a Roma*. She palmed the air and replied, 'I don't know Italian.'

'Let me help.' He linked her fingers in his. 'It says, 'She said yes in Rome.' I hope that wasn't too presumptuous. You see, I realised on this trip I always loved you and I still do, and I don't want to lose you again. When I thought you could be in danger, it mattered above everything else. You were way more important to me than the ship or my job. I really can't give up and let you go a second time.'

She blinked back tears of surprise at the heartfelt confession. 'I thought I'd lost you too.'

'You'll never lose me again. I'm here for keeps if you'll have me, Libby. And I'm pretty good at sticking to the course when I'm sure of journey's end.'

'Drew — I love you back. I can't even bear the thought of this cruise concluding; it's been magical. But most of all, the inspiring memories have come from you.'

'Then marry me. The tattoo was pretty painful; I hope it'll have the happy ending it deserves.' He grinned at her. 'We've just begun, but we're a safe bet. And if you're not convinced, take time to think about the wedding. Just keep it as an open suggestion. Something said in full passion beside a fountain in Rome. And if we need to come back again to get your answer, then we will. That too is doable. If this tattoo is misguided, it's going to take work to cover it up.'

'I know my answer. It's a yes! Though I do think you're crazy. Lovely crazy, but still prone to scary behaviour.' She smiled up at him, and knew she'd found her one true match. It shone from him like sunlight. 'I couldn't love you more.'

'Navigation co-ordinates in perfect synch. Let's go and sit down. Let me just hold your hand for a while and enjoy having you back by my side.'

'I'm relieved you said that. This ankle is still not up to lengthy standing.'

'Let's go eat somewhere. I've some duties on ship later as a wind up. What do you say we go up on deck and have a solo night we both deserve?' He bent down to steal a light, chaste kiss that was a promise of much more later.

She lingered in his arms, then pushed him back. 'Yes, please. I thought cruises were all about relaxing. Not criminals around every corner.'

'Life with me is never dull.'

And with no more words and only direct action, Drew turned her around in his arms and pulled her to kiss him.

'It's fun when you're no longer on duty . . . ' she whispered softly as his lips slid over hers and told her his words were in earnest. The caring true emotions in the man were ably demonstrated in that chaste but heart-felt fathom-deep kiss, while tourists gently applauded.

He laughed and she looked around to see Zak and Janna watching from a nearby café, Janna's gelato spoon held before her mouth. Zak leaned over to steal her food.

At a café right opposite them sat more familiar faces: Carl Lazlo and his daughter Lilly with Walt and Edna. She noted Lilly was attracting wishful looks from the local Italian scooter boys already. Her father would be on his toes with her. Correction; she could more than stick up for herself.

'Let's go see your friends. This is what's known as a champagne moment,' Drew urged.

And without further objection, she followed direct orders.

★　★　★

Cinderella underrated being the belle of the ball — or maybe the understudy — with all the dressed-up sparkle. Libby's bridesmaid's dress was quite a creation. But then, what else did she expect from a fashionista best friend like Chrissie?

It had been a show-stopper of a stately home wedding with an evening of twinkling champagne glass towers, divine foods, dancing, singing and performances all masterminded by the party-diva bride.

'And may I say I highly admire your plus-one,' Chrissie told her, planting yet another kiss on her cheek. 'I only wish he'd come dressed as captain.' Then

Chrissie self-corrected. 'Sorry. Apologies. Your fiancé. Please say you'll let me dance with him next? It's very mean of you to hog all the fun.'

'Trust me, we had a long journey to finally get one-to-one time. It took a whole cruise to work out the kinks.'

'You really must tell me all later. You are one lucky girl.'

Chrissie grabbed Drew's arm and pulled him to the dance floor before he could make excuses. He soon swept her into a waltz while Libby laughed and watched them.

She couldn't wait for her new life to start. Persuading Drew to take the new Far Eastern post hadn't been easy, but she'd won him around when she'd said she'd go too. More especially when she'd found out they needed a legal consultant. This way she got her travel wish and a new vocation off the ground. It was only a temporary contract, but with so much travel involved she'd be crazy to say no. It had seemed like fortuitous destiny. And it would do for starters.

His maiden voyage would be preparation, while this wedding would help her to prepare for another big day ahead. She fancied saying 'I do' with a sea breeze in her veil, and Sienna, Zak, the Randalls and all the special people she'd grown to love there. The romance of a cruise proved pretty hard to beat.

Libby sighed, smiling happily while recognising she was one lucky passenger. Despite false starts, they'd found destiny's true course.

We do hope that you have enjoyed reading this large print book.

Did you know that all of our titles are available for purchase?

We publish a wide range of high quality large print books including:
Romances, Mysteries, Classics
General Fiction
Non Fiction and Westerns

Special interest titles available in large print are:
The Little Oxford Dictionary
Music Book, Song Book
Hymn Book, Service Book

Also available from us courtesy of Oxford University Press:
Young Readers' Dictionary
(large print edition)
Young Readers' Thesaurus
(large print edition)

For further information or a free brochure, please contact us at:
Ulverscroft Large Print Books Ltd.,
The Green, Bradgate Road, Anstey,
Leicester, LE7 7FU, England.
Tel: (00 44) **0116 236 4325**
Fax: (00 44) **0116 234 0205**

NOT INTO TEMPTATION

Anne Hewland

Rejected by local landowner Sir George Foxcroft, Hannah Brockley opens a girls' school in the family home to achieve financial security for herself and her sister Margaret. But then one of the older pupils dies in suspicious circumstances. Both the sympathetic Reverend William Woodward and the handsome Dr Shipley were present that night. Will they help Hannah through a perilous spiral of danger and deceit to find the happiness she seeks — or could one of them be implicated in the crime?

FALLING FOR A STAR

Patricia Keyson

Thea loves her job in TV, but hates her boss Hermione. When Thea gets a chance to interview her favourite movie star, Justin Anderson, Hermione is willing to do anything to sabotage the blossoming romance between her underling and the handsome actor. Then Thea gets the chance to stay in Justin's country mansion and do some in-depth research. But is he really as nice as he seems? And will she become just another one of his easy conquests?

THE POTTERY PROJECT

Wendy Kremer

Commissioned to assess the Midland Pottery Company's financial prospects, Craig Baines faces an angry manager — Sharon Vaughan has had no warning of his arrival. The workforce soon accepts their well-meaning visitor, even though they know his findings could result in dismissals. When Craig detects that someone is pinching china and pitches in with Sharon to help solve the crime, she becomes increasingly aware of her attraction to him. But after his report is complete and he's about to leave, has she left it too late to let him know?

A SURPRISE ENGAGEMENT

Pat Posner

Flora can't understand how she let her best friend, Val, persuade her to pretend to be engaged to Val's brother, Bryce Torman, heir to the Torman estate. It's only supposed to convince their Uncle Hector that Bryce is serious about someone other than the singing star, Jilly Joy, he's recently been spotted with. To make matters worse, Flora and Bryce have got on like chalk and cheese since childhood — and yet Flora finds herself enjoying his 'fake' kisses rather more than she ought to . . .